The Days of Daniel

Life of the Lowly

The Book Title Copyright © 2021 IndieImprint

Published by IndieImprint

ISBN: 978-1-7366831-0-1

INTRODUCTION

Who is Daniel?

Well, he's no Rocket Scientist or one of them big shot Movie Stars. And he's certainly no Doctor, nor one of them Rich Lawyer types, nope. Daniel is just a good ole' fashion Lowly.

But what's a Lowly? Well that's what this book's all about: the life of one, the life of me, Daniel, a Lowly that is. The 'low low,' if you will. The Lowly is a spectacular creature filled with superstition and religion, and this book documents the thoughts and philosophies occupyin' one such critter. Now, this Lowly account can only be considered "based on a true story" and nothing written here should be considered more than fiction itself.

For most of the low life is undocumented and is experienced orally, so I will try my best to recount this lore as it has been passed down, mouth by mouth and deed by deed.

And to be honest...I just got downright tired of reading all those rich people writing the same books over and over.

Always going on about how to be a "better person," "make more money," or "how great they are" and "how to kick ass." They lack reality! The true Lowly life.

They're always talkin' about waking up on time and working hard! Well, I don't put much stock in that, and I ain't ever had no luck in it either! OHHHHH! the hassle, what about a little leisure reading for once?! So, if it helps, don't even consider this a 'book' – that's what people with "rules" make you read. Just consider this the longest text message you ever got! And perhaps it'll be more useful.

Dedication

To My Readers, I give you my heart.

Acknowledgments

To my love Kaela, my best friend and biggest supporter.

The Jezebel Spirit

To first understand "The Jezebel Spirit," one must consider what it means to have the "spirit" of something inside you. Most of us understand when people are "free spirits" or, during the holidays, someone may have a "Christmas Spirit."

When you have a "spirit" of something inside you, this will determine the way you act. I say that today there is a new "Spirit" amongst us: The Jezebel Spirit.

Maybe better understood as being "Narcissistic" or being a "Succubus." The Jezebel's strongest characteristics include being selfish and manipulative and having no empathy for others. The difference between them and a pure narcissist is the hint of evil that went into their soul when they were created.

A "Jezebel" feeds on the energy of people around them and there is no limit to the amount of energy they can suck from the room. You may have may have heard them referred to as "attention-whores."

While often Jezebels are women, there is a small percentage of male Jezebels in the population; you may have heard them referred to as "fuck boys."

A good Jezebel knows the most efficient way to harvest energy from others, and that is through those whom they can control the most. The path of least resistance. They don't waste time on those who don't succumb to their charm or give them what they desire.

They will push and pull their lovers in and out. One day loving them, one day hating them. One day making them feel unstoppable, only to bring them down with insults and embarrassment the next day. Constantly back and forth in a manipulative dance– like rolling a piece of dough, until they can mold their victim into whatever shape they desire.

Often the beauty and lustful ways of the Jezebel are too hard to resist and, before a man knows it, he's paying her cell phone bill and taking little Billy out to the batting cages. The Jezebel is often in relationships, but that is only to ensure they have a constant source of energy from which they can tap.

Most people call this a "boyfriend" or "girlfriend" but a Jezebel just calls it a reliable energy source. Like their own personal water well, they can draw from this source whenever they want and if they decide that the remaining charge is low or boring them, they head into public to find a greater source. Hall and Oates famously wrote a song about a fully charged Jezebel known as "Maneater," for example.

While I had battled my fair share of thots and heavily

medicated woman, it was only once that I truly encountered a full-fledged Jezebel demon.

By random chance, I had become gym buddies with a famous rapper's brother. His reputation seemed to proceed him wherever he went. One night we were talking, and SHE showed up from nowhere. She didn't know me, but she knew him, and I sensed she wanted to put a spell on him, but he was used to this kind of tactic, and didn't even budge. But that's how I met her. She was trying to hang with the cool kid, and I just so happened to be there when her poison ivy landed on my lap.

I should have known that there were red flags the first week we went out – I got a call from Detroit paramedics shortly after saying they had found her passed out downtown with no recollection of where she belonged, and now they were calling the most recent number on her phone...me.

Over time, as I would come around her apartment more often, I would encounter random dudes in the parking lot, lingering and watching her place like stalkers. They were like the ghosts of horrors past - souls she had taken who could never leave her be. They all gave me gloomy warnings of the future and a relationship headed for doom each one telling me their fatal story and how she had ruined their life, but I didn't believe anything they said about...*my girl.*

There is something to be said about the girl who wants to be the "hottest bitch" in the Golden Corral but still has no problem sneaking a few biscuits out in her purse. It didn't matter if we were surrounded by low-lows eating greasy buffet chicken, or if we were in an old persons' home visiting her grandmother. Every situation was a chance to get all eyes on her.

11

It was a mystery how she paid her bills. I even accused her

of stripping, but one of the ghosts had told me it was the other sugar daddies in the shadows that she still secretly had under her spell. *They would say anything to break us up, wouldn't they!*

The Jezebel's main weapon is her lust and beauty. They have the type of energy that means simply talking to them can excite and radiate a person, eventually winning them round, even if they already suspect the true intention is to use that beauty to manipulate.

Yet, while she controlled everyone, the demon that controlled her, at the top of the chain of command, was alcohol. She was forever drunk, and forever wearing makeup. I am not sure if to this day I ever saw her break character.

What I learned the hard way was that the Jezebel does not reason or do anything other than what they want to do. This is the result of having no empathy combined with a high degree of selfishness and mine had maxed out these attributes.

She told me she wanted to go get a drink one night, and so we did. But after "a" drink, I was ready to go. I always had work in the morning.

On this night though, the demon inside her was not ready to go; rather, it wanted to stay and drink more.

No matter what I did or said, nothing was going to change her mind, in fact, quite the opposite. Each request to leave the bar enraged her more until eventually she became so furious and obnoxious that it was I who left in a fit myself.

I sat at home for about 15 minutes and stewed about what had taken place. I was done. This was unbelievable...*had I met my match?*

I then decided that I would not be undone so easily, and so I went back to the bar, in a different outfit this time to get the evidence that she was the cheater that I thought she was. She said she wanted to stay and "dance." Well, I was going to come back and catch her red handed. That would show her.

When I returned to the bar (in a different outfit), I made a low-profile entrance and slipped into a seat where I could watch the dance floor.

Then I saw it, her dancing like an 80s jazzercise instructor on the dance floor. Her head bobbed up and down as she flipped her hair and gyrated her hips while jumping all around. She had so much energy from the souls she was harvesting in the room and everyone was watching...*my girl.*

My God! Was I becoming a ghost of Jezebels past? I could feel myself dissipating as I was now becoming one of the lost lingering, stalking souls that followed her.

Three girls sat down at the table and tried to have small talk with me, but I didn't care what they had to say. I was hypnotized by the snake's belly dancing.

After a while, she got tired, and I watched her move towards the bar. Like any good Jezebel, none of their actions goes without payment. Her little dance show for the bar brought her showers of free shots and she took each one...**with pleasure.**

Out of the trance, and without my blinders on, I now saw that the group that was handing her the shots was a gang of old and rough bikers. They laughed and jeered at their entertainment, paying her performance, and she loved it. She must have thought she was in some Sons of Anarchy movie.

Well, I wouldn't stand for it.

I headed to the dance floor and it was time to end this little charade. She was technically my "girlfriend" but now I know "words" mean nothing to demons. I told the old biker boys to saddle up and stand down.

Me and my girl were leaving.

They had their little fun, but now the show was over. They hated hearing that and they all looked at her. The Jezebel Spirit realizing it was about to lose a huge source of energy (and free drinks) reacted quickly. And that's when she said:

"I don't fuckin' know this guy!"

To be fair, it was a genius move. She jerked her wrist away from me and that was all the bikers needed to surround me. A sea of leather made a wall, with her on the other side. *She must have been a powerful demon to assume control of this biker gang so quickly, I thought.*

I went off on these bikers. I told them they were "fuckin' lucky" we were inside and dished out a few other threats while they looked at me like I was crazy to challenge them. I left with a big "fuck you" and middle finger in their face...they wanted to race ME to the bottom? These pretty boys with their leather and nice motorcycles?

I left the dance floor and went back to my stalking post. Shortly after, one of the bikers approached me. He said that

I had talked to their leader the wrong way, and now I would have to answer for my words. That I had to be dealt with for my "hard ass" showmanship the real way.

"Bring it!" I told him. He's been working for the Jezebel for what, a few hours? I was ready to die for my commander and if he thought I would break my allegiance so easily, then he must not have known what type of powerful spell I was under.

He stepped back and looked at my crazy eyes and he must have sensed her magic on me, because all of a sudden, he believed me.

He believed it was *my girl* and that she was lying. Now he understood. He told me, "If it really is your 'old lady,' she'll be home tonight. Don't worry about it and if not, then you know you can move on."

Pretty reasonable, I thought, so I apologized to him, bought him and his leader a beer, and went home to sleep. I decided I was done with her.

A few hours later, at 3 AM, just like the old biker oracle predicted, I heard her knocking. Furious knocking as if from hell...it was irregular and without pattern the knock of a demon. Like a scary movie, I hid under my blankets and wished it away. It seemed like the knocking went on for an eternity until slowly, it faded away.

Fifteen minutes later my phone began to furiously ring. Over and over, it rang. And rang. And rang. The demon had transformed its energy and was now attacking me through the Black Mirror. Assault on all fronts. I silenced it and hoped for a few hours of rest before work. And that's when the images came through. The pictures of bloodied, cut wrists. The text

15

messages that said it was my fault. My fault she had to become a cutter.

She told me before that if she couldn't have me, then she would kill herself.

She reminded me of this through text messages and told me this is why she tattooed my name on her arm.

Ohhhh, I see…it was time for the big pull. At first, she pushed me away at the bar, and now she would do anything to pull me back in under her control again.

I wasn't sure if it was illegal for me to ignore the fact that she was about to kill herself, even though the pictures looked like they were from a bad Google search.

A part of me really wondered if she would really hurt herself. She said she if she couldn't have me, then she would rather die…*prove you weren't always a liar!*

Still, I responded to her bloody wrist text message and told her to come back over.

When she came back to my apartment for the second time, there again, I heard it. The furious banging of hell again. This time, when I looked through the eye hole to confirm she hadn't cut herself, I could see she had opened my car doors and the lights were on and windshield wipers swiping. *Had the demon somehow Christine'd my car? Did she somehow bring this machine to life to kill me also? Imbuing everything she touched with some kind of Frankensteinesque animation life force, that was bent on carrying out her destructive will? No…I just left my car unlocked - but still.*

It was a scary sight peering in the night through the looking glass. I told her we were done, and I just wanted to see that she didn't kill herself. This enraged her and she banged even harder until a light bulb went off in her head. I watched her through the eye hole slowly calm down and back away.

Hauntingly, she somehow looked me directly in the eye, through the hole, and softly said, "OK. I'm going to call the police."

In a flash, she was back downstairs, in my car and smashing the horn. She showed no concern or remorse for the people sleeping all around the apartment complex. Then...she called the police. *My God! What kind of monster had I brought upon my neighbors!?*

Still watching through my peep hole, I saw the flashing of the cherry police lights roll up and could see her downstairs talking to them. From her exaggerated movements and mannerisms, I could see she was really going all in on the "damsel in distress" act. *I've seen it a million times.*

I watched in horror as she weaved her spell over the law enforcement officers and now the cops just as easy as the bikers were under her spell and under her command, and willingly ready to do her bidding - against me.

I watched them through the eye hole power up to the third floor. I stepped away from the door and a few moments later, I heard a different kind of banging. This banging had consistency. The tempo had rhythm, it was the banging of law and order. I knew that for this banging, I could not speak solely through the eye hole; for this one I'd have to reveal a bit of my face.

I opened the door behind a chain lock, just enough so I could stick half my eye outside, and said, "Is there a problem, officers?"

They explained to me that we needed to talk. That the girl downstairs said I was keeping her hostage in my apartment...

HOSTAGE IN MY APARTMENT?

WHAT!? DAMN! She was good. *Real good.*

She showed them bruises on her calf and told a story of how she had fought for her life up there. She said she was on the ground clawing at the carpet, while I held onto her legs trying to keep her in my apartment, then by her own prowess she got up, ran out, and escaped.

I stepped outside and explained to them that on the contrary, she hadn't stepped inside at all. I explained all the theatre that had been unfolding after we went out for "a" drink. I even showed them the bloody wrist picture. The demon never considered evidence.

Quickly, they snapped out of her spell and I asked them, *"Do you not see how drunk she is?"* They looked at each other and said they would come back after they corroborated their story. *Good luck, boyos,* I thought, as they turned on their heels for round two with the demon.

I shut my door and watched them walk downstairs back to her. They lost a little pep in their step suspecting that 'the big bust on a woman beater' was really a dud.

She melted once the interrogations turned on her and as the sun began to break, I stepped outside to hear the final questioning. I could tell she was tired from not getting her way and was quickly running out of energy. That's when she screamed at the cops.

She was now accusing them of sexual harassment. Saying they were trying to "have their way with her." The cops stood frozen and dumbfounded. *Welcome to my world, boys.*

I shouted down to them, "Told you so!" Just to take what little "bravado" they had left.

That's when I saw her glowing eyes look up and pierce me through the fading darkness. Hunched over, she hissed, "Seeee...yoooouuuuu" and she began to take off running. A few more steps down the sidewalk and a few more dreadful words hissed out "morrrrrrowwwwwww."

The cops stood frozen like stone as if they had just dealt with Medusa herself. The Jezebel wasted no time and through the breaking sunlight, her long black hair flowed like a shadow behind her, like a cape flailing in the wind, as she moved farther away from the crime scene. Each step seeming to move her faster and faster...faster than I had ever seen a normal human move. Galloping into the darkness.

It was only by chance that I caught a glimpse of moonlight hit her day-old make-up, revealing her face for the first time.

Her skin was wrinkled and weathered, and her eye fake lashes and fake hair were falling off. Her skin wasn't the tan it appeared – under the makeup, it was a greyish-ghoulish color and even her eyebrows were melting away to show the hideous creature underneath.

"Perverts!!" her screams rang out, fading away further

now though until finally, over a fire hydrant, around a tree, and past the last set of apartment buildings, she disappeared out of sight.

It was done now. The demon was gone, but with no time to sleep, I dreadfully drove to work with no energy. All morning long I thought about what the creature had said to me, what hex or curse she chanted in my name - when it hit me at lunch.

"Seeee you tomorrow night!" Yes...that's what it said.

The Bakers Dozen

When I graduated from college, besides being the first in my family to do such a feat, I did like most other collegiate dreamers and moved back home with my parents. So much for college being a ticket to the better life.

At the same time, my older brother, who'd recently ended a long-term relationship, decided he too would drop in for a 'short' stay as well to make it a full family reunion. Baggage and worldly possessions in hand. It was in these circumstances, after living happily together for years without children, that my parents found themselves with two grown men suddenly back in the nest.

Life appeared to resume well. At first, it was just like old times. But it only took a few months for me to realize something horrible was happening. My mom was cheating on my dad.

Or so I would come to accuse her.

All I can piece together correctly was, during my last few years at school, Mom occasionally mentioned she had a new friend. A baker friend. She'd mention it in passing, when sharing recipes or recommending the best temperature to cook a pizza. That sort of thing. There was no reason for us to question this, or even give it a second thought; Mom always had a knack for befriending people and my parents really liked their sweets.

Once, I had personally come to know one of my mom's old, Italian, bakery lady friends who gave us sweets for free. Granted, it was only the old stuff, always the stale goodies that were going to be thrown away...*but hey, beggars can't be choosers.*

However, fast-forward many years later, when I moved back home, and one of the first changes I noticed was the fridge was always full of the most beautiful Italian pastries. All the pastries you could imagine: Biscottis, Sfogliatella, Cannoli, and all kinds of other foods I can't spell.

None of this could be described as the 'stale shit' either. No off-cuts, no throwaways, and no failed baking experiments. This was the good stuff.

Freshly made, and one hundred percent delicious.

So far, so scrumptious. Until one day, when I walked into the house, I heard my mom on the phone: **"I love you,"** she said to someone before hurrying to get off her cell phone. This was interesting, I thought, because my dad and brother were outside – who else could she be so in love with?

22

From the type of family that doesn't say 'I love you' or show much affection at all, this was weird. She hastily went back to doing the dishes and I walked in the kitchen to get some food. For now, consider my suspicions fully aroused.

When I opened the fridge, there they were again: the Biscottis, Sfogliatellas, Cannoli, and all kinds of other foods I can't spell.

Day by day the kitchen was quickly turning into some kind of never-ending, automatically refilling, Italian bakery. More Italian pastries than you could imagine were falling out of our fridge and pantry. All fresh and all delicious. And you know what I thought?

What kind of fucking 'friend' would make you all this food every day?

Out of the goodness of their heart? Come on. There was more to this!

This wasn't just someone overestimating the Frittuli they'd need on a Saturday and sharing the leftovers. This stank of deceit, adultery, and for now, good chocolate too.

When I opened the fridge, it immediately didn't feel right, and trust me, this wasn't Dad's leftover lasagna either. The energy from the food hit me like a dark wave, and at that moment I was in no doubt about what was going on. It was like the buttery croissant reached out to me and whispered, "Son" (with an air of arrogance that only a delicate piece of pastry could muster), "your mom's fucking my creator." I was furious, both at my mom and that imaginary croissant.

I waited until my mom left her cell phone alone. She didn't

have a password or anything because she paraded herself as 'the golden standard,' impeccable in every way. Who would really think the good old respectable Catholic lady might be up to no good? That she might have anything to hide? No one ever had a reason to check her phone...but I did.

Unfortunately, my suspicions were confirmed. There it was in black and white: five calls to the same number in the last two days. Including one around the time I'd overheard the "I love you."

I looked for a phone number in her recent calls around the time she would have been saying those unfaithful words, those words that could bring a family crumbling down, and I called that number back.

A man's voice answered "HELLLOOOO" like a chipper Wayne Newton, thirstily awaiting a call from his mistress. I blew up: "WHO THE FUCK IS THIS?"

The coward didn't even say a word, then he hung up. I knew who it was though. It was the fuckin' Baker, that's who!

Every time we called back; he ignored the call. I only ever heard his voice once, and I say 'we' because it was a hard pill for my brother to swallow. He hadn't dealt with the savagery of females as readily as I had. Even though I told him earlier in the day that the evidence was starting to unfold, he didn't believe it. He had that "Mom? Really?" face.

Yes. Mom. Really.

Looking back, I don't blame him though – it's hard for us to see our parents as anything but perfect. We don't want to see them as anything BUT perfect; however, a huge part of

24

understanding this life is understanding your parents' struggles.

Understanding that they are people too and not perfect. And like all imperfect people, they are flawed.

Deep down, we still wish them to be perfect, to live up to our expectations. But they don't. They have their own desires, dreams, and issues. Some will be addressed. Others won't.
They just try and do their best like the rest of us.

Anyway, I brought forth an ultimatum to my mom. She needed to tell Dad, or I would. She became very defensive and made it clear she was not willing to negotiate or admit to the crimes accused.

Consequently, I had no choice. I walked into my dad's room, where he was sleeping, and I flicked the lights on and off to wake him up. I then told him everything and explained to him the conspiracy at hand.

He asked my mom to see her phone, but surprise, surprise, she had already cleared it of all messages and calls.

The lack of evidence was all he needed to not believe.

He faked being mad for about 15 minutes before going back to bed. There was always work in the morning.

I couldn't believe my parents. The ones who taught me everything about morals and how to treat people right were now taking massive shits on each other.

Suuuuuuure, I knew my dad wasn't the golden standard, but MOM? I thought Mom was the high integrity person she painted herself to be. How fooled she had me, her own son.

How could my dad just turn a blind eye though? And my mom...how could she betray the family unit?

I know even to this day that my brother and my dad have forgotten, but I never have and sometimes I find myself making excuses for my mom. Acting like what I discovered wasn't true or saying that "affairs happen."

I could hear my dad's voice in my thoughts saying, "The poor thing...at least she picked someone who gave to the family."

In her own little twisted way, maybe she thought she was doing the family a favor by getting us the desserts we all loved.

My dad used to brag about working the most in the shop: 90 or even 100 hours a week. This is what got him excited. What he never stopped to realize was that all that time he was at work was time my mom spent alone. A classic recipe for a desperate housewife deprived of attention. *I've seen it a million times.*

Isn't it funny how many men start working for the love of their family - but end up only loving their work? Over time, they just love work in which they lose the love of their family, and they forget why they started it all in the first place. *It's a funny direction love can take you.*

In the end, whatever the conspiracy was that I had to say, it wouldn't matter though; because my dad would always forgive Mom for anything.

It was the kind of unconditional love that I couldn't understand yet, and even though I learned the lesson, it was something I could not live with. Two weeks later I moved out.

My parent's said I was over-reacting and that I had made it all up in my head, when one day, I got a phone call from the same number I seen in my mom's phone. *I could not believe she had given him my number.*

When I answered, I heard "HELLLOOOO" like a chipper Wayne Newton. I blew up: "WHO THE FUCK IS THIS?"

"ITSA' ME!" he chirped.

"From Paisano's Bakery & Cakes" he said even louder as if I couldn't hear him.

"You-ah, wanted me to call-ah, when your cake-o was done?" he now said confused.

My jaw dropped and my head started to spin. Slowly I mustered up enough courage to ask him two questions.

"Does the cake have writing on it?" I dreadfully ask.

"Yes, yes" he says excitedly in his thick Italian accent.

"What does it say?"

"The birthday cake says: **'I love you'**... just like the lady ask me to put down a few weeks ago!"

Power of the Word

When I was in college, there was a small religious man who used to stand on campus and preach against the students. And anyone else unlucky enough to walk by and get caught in the firing line.

He picked a good spot in between all the main buildings; the changing classes meant he always had a constant flow of people passing or circling him.

He said things like, "God hates fags" and "Sinners are going to Hell." He said that we were all "drunks", "whores", "liars," and "cheats" – the works. He used all the standard religious hate speech we've now come to know and love.

One of my favorite insults, though, was that we were "Central Masturbators University" creative, I thought.

It didn't matter if people would try and debate with him or try and reason with him, he always answered in semi biblical ways that didn't really make sense to anyone. I, like many other students, had started to recognize his regular schedule and as the weeks would pass, it became a regular freakshow.

I should clarify too that I wasn't one of those religious nuts either, because there were Christian fraternities and sororities on campus that I laughed at. One Christian fraternity used to give out free hotdogs every Friday. They were known as "Jesus Dogs." They did that because sobering up the drunk kids was the right thing to do...no wonder they hated this guy.

As the weeks passed, so did the tolerance of the students. Counter protests appeared regularly and often people just stood next to him, shouting random noises at the top of their lungs, just to drown out his voice and whatever he had to say.

Then one day as the crowd was really getting fired up, and the man continued in his biblical tongues, a guy on his bike rode through the circus of people and spat right on the man. The big loogie he hawked up landed square on the preacher's shoulder, and as the biker held his head high, he just kept pedaling and muttering some of his own words too, as he served some 'nice vigilante justice of his own on that religious freak.'

Everyone in the crowd, myself included, did not do or say anything as he rode off. It was clear that a new enemy had appeared on campus and, as the days passed, the lines were drawn: him vs. everyone else. It didn't matter – black, white, man, woman, gay, straight, fat, skinny. Everyone that gathered at these semiweekly spectacles was unified in their hate of this man.

But you know what?

He was right.

He spoke our truths.

I always think about the radicalness or even ridiculousness of what he used to say, but maybe it was the realness. We wanted to surround ourselves with people who agree with everything we do and make us feel comfortable, the people that tell us, "Hey, not everything's that bad." We loved this American life and our American ways, yet the truth remained: we were masturbators, drunks, cheaters and, by biblical definition, sinners.

I know because I lived amongst them, I was one of them. Still am.

Surely not everyone was like this but college for me was always a place to go partying, and everything I knew from TV or learned from people before me was that it was the place to party.

The harder you partied, the cooler it was. What douche went to study?

We chased the drunkenness, the whorishness, the lying, the freak nasty shit. That's what we loved, the debauchery.

I definitely didn't go to college to be conservative and worship Jesus, but the religious freak was right when he called it like it was. Truth hurts, huh?

I was a low life, surrounded by other people of low standards and morals. It was obvious by our actions of drunkenness and the whorishness of which we stood accused.

Over time I started to think the line in the sand was not drawn by the student body but rather by that small preacher guy himself.

Everyone wanted to hate him, but they never considered that he hated them back.

I am not saying his practice or delivery was right, but it was damn effective! And wasn't it funny though that these people who were so desensitized by everything else could be so bothered by this random guy on the sidewalk... speaking some words?

I mean, how else was he to approach such extreme people who were so desensitized, so insensitive, and so numb? What did the "kids" want? For him to talk "nice"?

These very college kids with dark minds who have seen horror movies where people get torn to shreds. These kids who have watched the most extreme forms of pornography, these kids who have done crimes, drink and do drugs. They got all butthurt by their own truths!

Why should he talk nicely to the young girl that calls her mom a "bitch" or the young man that tells his dad to "fuck off?"

Most people never listen to anything anyone has to say, but they listened to him. I had never seen anyone protest a movie they watched, spit on a movie director, or even yell at a journalist, but boy, did they hate him!

That's when I started to understand the power of the word. Specifically, the power of the word when spoken in truth.

As demons hate the words of God, so do the demons within

people.

That is why so many people detest hearing scripture.

Day in and day out, that little 'religious freak' took the abuse of the circus. There was no gain to his practice. There was no attentive congregation lining up to enter his 'radical hate church.' Nonetheless, all the shouting and negative energy, arguing, and even spitting did not stop him. Every day he came out there to face the masses who just generally wanted him gone. Nobody wanted to hear it, even if we needed to.

It did not matter the amount of people against him; every time he mustered up the same vigilance as before, and every time I went, I noticed he would hold a Bible under his arm.

He held onto that old book like a running back would carry a football. It didn't take a genius to see it was the Bible that gave him strength.

It was always my thought that college should be a place where you learn anything. I was always interested in what everyone said, even if I didn't agree, and now, I had to know more about this book. How could it make one man strong enough to go against 50 people?

Today, college kids are indoctrinated, not educated. They're carbon copies and zombies to whatever mainstream propaganda says is 'normal,' and Christianity is NOT normal...

In the end though he was right about us, and we were also right about him. We were sinners but he was radical!

And to some level that was his final lesson to me. That radicalness is what it takes to be a Christian. To maintain your faith despite every challenge.

When the world wants to carry on or encourages you to follow the masses, the person that tries to STOP them would HAVE be different. The person that merely brought it up would have to be hated!

The catch is: you would have to be a little radical and extreme to carry on when there's nothing to gain and the world wants you to stop.

This is as true today as it was when Jesus walked.

That year I picked up every free "handout" Bible I had seen tossed on the ground around campus - tossed out by the students who were friendly enough to take them from the 'Jesus Freaks,' but secretly didn't want them. I still have two of them next to my bed where I sleep.

Cats on a Ledge

My little condominium does not have any screens in the windows. Now, when I open the windows, both my cats like to walk outside on the windowsill.

Naturally, I worry about this and I always call for them to come back inside, but even if they were to fall, it would only be a short fall onto soft dirt, a fall that would not hurt them.

My oldest cat, Moe, is a scaredy-cat. A real 'pussy,' you might say. Even though I call for him to come back inside the window, deep down I don't really worry about him jumping or falling off. He is extra cautious and makes sure he never slips on that ledge.

It is my all-black alley cat, Neo, on the other hand, that worries me. For Neo, the black cat is different than Moe, the-scaredy-cat. I sense his soul yearns for a life of adventure. I

34

feel he would have a more satisfying life in the wild, as a street cat, even though neither he nor I know what that looks like.

Unlike Moe, Neo's not scared of the sounds of random birds or lightning. He likes to eat all kinds of bugs and any food you feed him. He even tries to sneak out through the garage, and car rides are adventures he's always willing to set out on.

For Neo, beyond the windowsill is a life of adventure, all the bugs he could eat, and all the new trees he could climb. He stares at the birds, not with hunger in his eyes, but with jealousy of their freedom. For him, the world passing by that window is never ending satisfaction.

For Moe, I know he will never jump because there is nothing out there for him. I know him, and the prospect of cold nights or rainy days does not appeal to him. He likes to be here. His meals, his naps, he enjoys the safety of our home, and for that he is always welcome here. Maybe his glory days are behind him, maybe his youth too. He now looks to spend the rest of his days without risk, in security, in comfort, inside.

I have come to understand that people are like both these cats.

Like Moe, some will always prefer safety and comfort, and that's fine. Society will always have a place for you. But for others, their world is like Neo's.

Maybe it is the fear of the unknown that makes you stay. Maybe you're scared to hurt yourself jumping. Maybe it is the love of your friends and family...whatever it is, you always stay where you are! What kind of fulfillment could one's soul have from a place outside of their comfort zone?

Now, when Neo gets on the ledge even though I tell him to come back, I secretly think to myself:

JUMP, NEO! JUMP!

Prove to me, little cat, that you can do it.
Prove to me, Neo, that you can jump into the unknown, so I can too.

The Jar

If I told you that I would pay you 500 dollars to work for me on a Saturday...for, say, eight hours, would you do it? Nothing heavy, just some basic computer work for eight hours?

Most people would say yes, emphatically. That is 62 dollars an hour!

I took a similar shittier deal like this many Saturdays in a row – my company called it "overtime."

Each overtime shift I would laugh to myself at how stupid the company was for letting me come in and do the same work for MORE money. I was getting one over on them, I thought.

Then one day, someone told me they had this 'jar,' and in it there was a green rock for every Saturday they thought they had left on Earth.

Every week one green rock was removed. It was a visual representation of how finite your time here on Earth really is. And as the green rocks were removed, you would see your limited life get even shorter.

I started thinkin' about people like Einstein, Hawking, and other big brained people who make these incredible equations to explain reality.

But, I thought, the average person can also make equations to explain our life.

The moment I heard about the Jar; the equation of MY life was clear.

If there are 52 Saturdays in a year and I get paid $500 overtime to work each of them, that's:
52 x $500 = $26,000 per year.

After 10 years, you could save $260,000 (after taxes, we will call it $200,000).

So now, what if I made you a different deal?

I want every one of your Saturdays for the next 10 years for $200,000.

Still only eight hours. Would you accept that deal? Some people would accept, but some people wouldn't. The equation just made it clear to me that while I thought I was getting one over on the corporation, they were getting one over on me by owning my life for relatively cheap.

Ask yourself how long you must work to get out of debt? Buy a new house? A new car?

You can't win the game of monopoly by going around GO and collecting every week. It's an impossible plan; you will always get hit with Chance incidents that drain your bank account.

So why would anyone make "working" the plan of their life? With a book, I can tell you exactly how many I'd have to sell to be out of debt. I CAN'T tell you how many Saturdays I must work to do the same though.

If I committed every single one of my Saturdays for the next 10 years to something, couldn't I make more than $200,000!?

What is wrong about my first equation though is that most people don't make 62 dollars an hour. So, let's make the equation for someone getting paid the US average minimum wage, working 40 hours a week.

$7.25 min wage x 8 hour work day = $58 a day
$58 a day x 52 working weeks = $3,016

I can legally buy every one of your Mondays for a year @ 3k – not bad. If I committed every single one of my Mondays for one year to something, couldn't I make more than 3k?

Talk about corporate slavery.

I will be telling you when you come in, when you can eat, when you take breaks, and when you leave. I don't care about how long it takes you to get here or to get home and I don't care about the weather, your family, your health conditions, or how much sleep you get or need because it's on my time and I own you now.

Not only that, but you must also come in every single

Monday for this deal to work, and Tuesdays and Wednesdays, Thursdays and Fridays!!

What is the price of your life and your time? What is the cost at which someone can own you? Instead of seeing the hourly rate or yearly rate, what is the cost of one hour of your life? What is the cost of your entire life?

To that, I say it's priceless.

Schadenfreude

As I set out to write these stories, I would be lying if I said I wasn't intimidated by all the great authors who came before me. All those long words and names they made up for their exceptional stories; I'd much rather speak in emoji.

All the eloquent sentences that flowed from their tongues and mind like honey, from comb to page. OHHHH NO! This wasn't me!

Still, I insisted to enter their realm. I would have to create my own words though, from "Hobbit" to "Lightsaber" to "Selfie." To be a creative writer meant…well, to be a creative writer! I needed to make my own words but that was no easy task indeed, and just to make up any ole' hobgobblish word wasn't worth my while. I wanted my word to have weight a word that could tell a tale! I wanted to add my own word to the dictionary like a chemist adds to the periodic table!

41

But...then like a flash of lightning, I had a new idea.

What if I just made-up new punctuation?! There are all kinds of words! But punctuation, now that was an exclusive group! And who was my competition?

The Mark Brothers: Exclamation and Question. Or the very juvenile Colon, and his younger (closely related) sibling, Semi. And OH, of course, THE DOTS.

One Dot .

Two Dot :

and Three Dot ...

...I could just do Four Dot :: and use it every time I break the rules of grammar ::

BAH HUMBUG! This damn "punctuation" group was even worse; they all seemed like a bunch of imbeciles if you ask me.

Never mind these old English snobs...no one's ever heard of them anyways! I decided...they can have their punctuation!

I went back to the drawing board to create a word that would forever change the world, to take mankind forward! In the same way that the invention of the steam engine brought the Industrial Revolution, my invention would bring about a new era. Expanding the ways humans communicate, and the ways they think!

Then another bright idea came to me... If I could not produce a word or punctuation, then what if I made the word...

TALLER!
What if... just what if...
I WROTE IN ALL CAPITAL LETTERS...
DAMNIT! NEVERMIND!
Or
Maybe add a little slant?
Or
WHAT IF I MADE THEM A LITTLE FATTER?
Too Bold? Or not bold enough?!
Or what if I chopped them in half!
LEGIT!
Or what if I made the words wider?!
Noooooooooooooooooooooooooooooo!
They did that too.

This was just tacky! People were just doing whatever they wanted with this language thing. And they wanna get mad if I start a sentence with But! But the audacity, I tell you!

Defeated and distraught, I wallowed about never having my word and I did what all quitters do: I went on YouTube, and like a flash of lightning my FINAL idea came to me as I watched dog videos on the tube.

In this one video the dog's owner walks in the door to find the dog has made a huge mess while the owner was gone. The dog has ripped through the old garbage can and torn the guts out of every feather pillow in sight. The dog has made a complete mess of the place.

Then the owner 'pretends' to be mad and says something like "DID YOU DO THATTTTTTTT?" or "WHOOOO DID THIS??" or "COCO, WAS THAT YOUUEWWWWW?"

The dog knows they are busted, and you can see the

shame and embarrassment on its face. Sometimes the dog is so ashamed it cannot even look you in the eye.

What the weird thing is though that everyone watching, including the dog's master, usually finds enjoyment in the animal's embarrassment or shame.

And this was my new word.

Ah, yes! There would now be a word for it!

What would I call someone who enjoyed watching others be embarrassed? What was the word for someone who enjoyed other's shame or guilt?

But lo, what light from yonder window breaks?! Thus, the dawning realization, glaring into my eyes, that MY word already exists: Schadenfreude

Them damn mother-loving Germans beat me to it.

Can you believe that the first word I made up in English was already made up in German and used in English for the same thing! How...confusing....how deflating...how redundant!

Like Edison inventing the lightbulb, only to emerge from his lab to see the hallway lit by Candle LEDs.

Oh yes, good ole' classic Schadenfreude.

Brain Damage

There is a reason we kiss and hug, you know, why we shake hands. And why sometimes you just gotta punch someone in the face.

Sometimes words are just not enough, and that's comin' from someone who wrote a book! Sometimes we need that physical contact to know it's real. Actions...well, actions speak louder than words, so they say.

Now, when it comes to fighting...a lot of people get in a street fight and they think it is going to be like the UFC or some MMA match, but in a street fight, there are no rules. It doesn't end when you want it to. There is no referee to step in and stop someone from getting hurt.

I'd say the only way for a street fight to end is someone gets hurt. Or it can be said, to win a fight, you must hurt someone.

This is not a good proposition for anyone and as time has gone on, I have learned to "walk away" from many fights.

Anyways, I had a friend who I'll call "Goofball," and one night he was mad that I was going to have girls over. To this day, I'm not sure why, other than he didn't like them. We always hung out with these girls, and while he was normally okay with them, on this night, for whatever reason, he did not want them at our place.

So, I figured Goofball was just being a crab, and had them come by anyways...

It should be noted that I had already learned my lesson about fighting before this night and when I sensed he was getting angry with me and as the situation was escalating, I did just "walk away."

I went onto the front porch and figured I could at least give him the house and the rest of us could hang out outside - since it was apparently such a big deal.

Still, Goofball wasn't okay with my little plan and being outside with the girls was pissing him off. After a little bit of time passed on the front porch, Goofball came outside with a bowl of cereal and before I could say anything, he was yelling and coming directly at me!

Next thing I know, he's throwing the bowl of cereal right at my face!

It flew in what seemed like slow motion, and from behind all the milk and little Cheerios flying through the air, I could see he was coming at me too...

His rage came at me so quick, so unexpected, that I naturally did what anyone would do. I put my hands up and shoved him back.

Nothing aggressive – I had punched other low-life's for less, and anyone caught off guard would put their hands up to try and stop something coming at them too!

And that's all it took.

Goofball was buzzed and uncoordinated, so what I didn't expect is that he would fall straight back like chopped timber and crack his head on the corner of the house.

He was knocked out before he hit the ground and without any motor function to support him, he hit his head one more time on the floor of our wooden porch.

Instantly he started seizing.

His mouth started foaming and he lay there on his side unable to breathe. He made exasperated gasps for air. His breaths were short, and he was totally unconscious.

A little bit of me died at that moment because I knew my life was over...*after Goofball died, that was.*

Of all the stupid shit that could be done, killing your friend was unfathomable. Who does that? I never heard about anyone doing that. *What kind of low-down, rotten, no-good Devil kills their roommate!?*

And by a freak accident...who would believe that? Yeah right, with my track record of fighting, I would be hung out to dry, and I didn't even mean for this to happen!

As he lay there seizing, I called 911! *Yes...me!*

I told them to send an ambulance and that my friend was dying. The operator asked what happened.

I said, "We got in a fight" and I hung up. Of course, they called back.

But the second time I just told the whole story how you just read it. What I didn't anticipate, and what I should have known, is that when the ambulance showed up, so did the cops.

I watched the paramedics save Goofball on that porch and they quickly took him away to the hospital while the Coppers started their questioning.

Everyone there on the porch, the girls included, saw what happened and that Goofball had come outside to try and fight me - *I was just defending myself!*

What shocked me though is that the girls or the cops really couldn't care less about the guy they'd just carted away.

After it was confirmed he was the 'bad guy,' everyone was ready to move on. In the eyes of the public, he got what he deserved.

Classic Schadenfreude.

The girls were ready to keep partying and the police officer forgot why he came there.

The girls kept saying things to this police officer like, "What are you doing later" and "Oh, a man in uniform," and for whatever reason, he couldn't care less about me.

Now I knew why Goofball didn't like these girls.

But that didn't change anything about Goofball's current state and that didn't mean that I didn't have a conscience either. It was still my roommate and my friend, and he was still on the way to the hospital over a freak accident.

The ride to the hospital seemed so long.

When I got there, I threw up all over the parking lot from the overwhelming anxiety of thinking about how I'd killed Goofball.

For hours we waited for the doctors to try and help him. When they came back, it was with the worst possible news.

He had brain damage and was bleeding from the brain.

They said they couldn't help him there and he would have to be taken to a University Hospital, about two hours away, in an ambulance where they could help him.

When it rains, it pours.

What I didn't know is that Goofball had about four or five previous concussions from playing other sports, which made him concussion prone. Light bumps or knocks to the head could put him out cold.

The docs told him that any more concussions after that night would be permanent brain damage.

Goofball is fine now and to this day, we continue to be friends. Even he laughs at how douchey the cereal bowl move was, though I'm sure ole' Goofball has his own version of the story, but the first time I met his mom, he said:

"Here, meet the guy that almost killed me." I say "said"...it was more of a slur...JK! Droolball's speech is totally unaffected.

Well, that is, unless he's got plans to throw more cereal at me.

"What's up, Motherfucker?"

Because the college I went to was on an Indian Reservation, that meant there was a casino right around the corner you could get into at 18 rather than 21, like most other places in the US. Obviously, this meant I was always skipping class to gamble. A 'gamble' in itself, you could say, that wasn't paying off, considering my grades.

I wasn't making any money listening to the professors and on a good run, I could easily scrape a few hundred bucks from the natives. I went there often but one day, I came across another young guy playing Blackjack. He was by himself and like me, he already beat the Five O'Clockers in.

The difference was he was severely disabled and bound to a wheelchair.

Nonetheless, it was one of those high-tech chairs (with a

sweet joystick to steer). Even moving the chips in and out between hands to bet was a hassle for him. By tapping the table or waving his arm right at the edge, he let the dealer know how he wanted to bet. He had no control over his legs or arms; pushing the joystick and his chips were about the extent of his control.

The dealer, staying true to his name, was well aware of the "deal" between them. The dealer moved his chips for him. He moved them in when he lost and moved them out when he won.

After a while, I started to notice the dealer almost never pushed chips back to him. When he won, he let it ride until he lost. Rarely did he have a large enough amount that satisfied him enough to bring it in. *I don't think the money mattered as much to him as it did to me.*

I started to wonder, who does more damage, a drug dealer or a card dealer? I haven't decided yet, but I think I trust drug dealers more.

Surprisingly though, I would see him soon again at the most popular bar on campus. I was shocked, as anyone would be, to see him taking shots of liquor with a group of hot girls.

Disabled in a wheelchair, one hot girl held his head back, while another poured a shot down his throat – was this legal?

He wiggled with excitement after each shot and took in huge puffing breaths of air. That was about all the noise he could make. His excitement radiated and from his sideways smile, you could tell he enjoyed having a good time.

Then I thought to myself, *this little bastard is getting all the attention!*

I wonder whether it was the off-road tires or the armrest that doubled as a seat for the girls. Whatever it was, I decided he liked Blackjack, he liked drinking, and he liked hot girls. We should team up. Now, when I say he liked to drink, I meant it. He liked to drink, and he was a regular at that bar.

From then on, when I saw him, he would puff huge breaths of air and wiggle like he usually did. Of course, we would take shots and shots and shots. So many shots that I was hoping I didn't kill this poor bastard. But hey, the ladies loved it and he had an advantage because he never had to worry about balance. He also didn't have to worry about drinking and driving.

On St. Patty's Day we had a party at my house and in typical fashion, I would leave the house, wander to other parties, and then come back to my house party.

Again, on that day, to my surprise, I saw him on "Frat Row," one of the most popular blocks on campus! *How did this guy know about all the hot spots?*

When he saw me, he laughed his sideways laugh and puffed in breaths of air - *as if he was surprised to see me!* The pretentious bastard!

After a little reminiscence and a few drinks on Main Street, I told him we should head home to my party, as surely, he would be a hit there too, and he grunted in a way I had come to understand as 'yes' in our common language.

As fate would have it, our house had a huge handicap-friendly porch with a ramp from the previous tenants, which could finally have its moment of usefulness.

After a while and many drinks, when the party was ending, like any good comrade, I offered to make the trek home with him, so he didn't have to go alone.

After about three or four miles, I started to get a little paranoid and tired myself. Then it occurred to me...

He doesn't even have to walk like I do!!

This all-terrain, highly sophisticated machine he was riding could go on for hours! I didn't have that kind of energy in my battery! And I had to go back the opposite way all by my drunken self.

So, I told him the deal and asked him if he could carry on the mission alone. He grunted in our common language and pushed forward. I'll never forget watching his chair pull away from me and, within a few minutes, he was already out of my sight! Surely moving faster than if I was walking with him. For someone who we called "disabled," he was seemingly "able."

Finally, my last year at college, I had a project to interview someone disabled in our community. I was friends with him on Facebook by this time and I reached out to him and asked if he wanted to do it.

When I showed up to *his* house that he owned, I was surprised again to see that he had a lady caregiver who did his daily tasks... *Where did it end with this Gatsby character!?*

As I walked in the living room, there he was sitting in his all terrain La-Z-Boy and he smiled and huffed a breath of excitement as he always did when he saw me.

54

But this time I heard something strange coming from his wheelchair...it sounded like the voice of a robot!

And it said:

WHAT'S. UP.
MOTH. ER.
FUCK. ER.

Ha! Now he could talk!! And what a way to greet an old friend!

His mouth was even dirtier than mine, or maybe he was a little salty still from me getting him a little too drunk.

He told me in his new robot accent that his "speaking board" had been out all this time. This technology was special and took a long time to get repaired. He showed me how he could press against a screen and have words and preloaded sentences ready to be said. He could connect to the internet, make a post on Facebook, and make phone calls. He even said things to me in French and Chinese! This bastard could speak 10 languages now... *I bet the ladies were going to love that!*

It was impressive how quickly he could navigate the tablet with just his knuckles. Just a testament to the fact that people take for granted what they are capABLE of doing. All the way down to their little fingertips.

He went on to tell me that the thing he missed most was his ability to post on Facebook and make status updates. Like all of us, he just enjoyed being connected, being heard. It was cool to see him happy, and for me...well, he had one last question to ask...

"CASINO?"

"CASINO. AFFIRMATIVE. OVER," I said back in my best robot voice.

The Negatives

I used to believe in this wall quote that said people are like the seeds of a plant – we all kind of start off as the same seed and we all have the same potential to grow. And if we are lucky enough to get love and light, and all the other necessary nutrients, we can grow to our maximum potential!

Sadly, some seeds can't grow because they are in the dark, not given any love or light. They are abused or they are neglected. Like a dark cloud, this trauma shadows over them and stops them from photosynthesizing, never allowing them to get any of the things a human seed needs to grow. The soil in which these seeds are planted is rotten and deficient. Literally, "soiled."

I believed that for a long while, but what no one ever told me is that there are some people that grow in the dark - on purpose.

Whether that be on the dark web, in a dark club, or dark alley, some people purposely try and develop in the dark.

Ironically, in photography, the pictures that are developed in the dark are called "The Negatives."

I say, stay away from The Negatives.

Those people who grow up in the dark, without light or water. They are planted in an infertile environment. Rejecting parental support and education.

Without the right tools, diet, a safe and secure home. Without these things, like many plants without the things needed to survive, they too fail to blossom, and instead wither. Tragically, they never get the chance to achieve their full potential. Although there are some who, despite this deficiency, learn to survive in the dark, they are forced to make up for the things they lack. They seek survival any way they can, even if that means resorting to illegal or immoral means. If they don't have enough water in their soil, they'll steal it from the neighboring tulip. They'll climb around the neighboring sunflower to achieve greater heights and fight for light. Some choose to be negatives and some have to be.

I say, stay away from The Negatives.

First Time I Smoked Weed

In 7th grade, like most other prepubescent dweebs, I started to think about how I liked the "pretty" girls. The problem was, I didn't hang out with or know any of them they only hung out with the cool kids.

I would have to become a "cool kid", I thought, and I plotted on how exactly I would do that.

I figured my best in was one friend who had another friend who was a "cool guy." Sometimes he would go with him to the cool kids' hangout and when I caught wind of them going, I knew I had to be there!

Over time I convinced them to bring me along with them to the "cool kids'" group where all the pretty girls hung out, and my mission was accomplished. My first time showing up at the cool kids' hangout, I was different. I wore Hawaiian shirts, and

I was tanner than the rest of them. The second time I hung out with them, one of the coolest girls said, "Danny again?" And since no one objected, I was there to stay. I became a regular in that group.

I was a cool kid.

Now, two years later going into 9th grade and high school, we would be combining with another local middle school. My two years as a cool kid were short-lived and I realized I would have to renew my status as "cool guy" once again. It was time for the little fish to enter the big pond we all knew as "High School."

I needed another plan for becoming a "cool kid." I plotted and schemed again and concluded that I should be cool with another "cool kid" from the other middle school! That would give me a contact in the rival group. So, at the beginning of that 9th grade year, a crucial time to establish order, I planned how to infiltrate yet another group.

I caught wind that one of the coolest kids from the other middle school was having a party. He was popular and he played football, which meant naturally he would rise in the pecking order I knew as popularity. I didn't play football, but girls loved football...I knew I had to be there!

His older brother in the 12th grade was an even more popular kid because he was the varsity high school football star. I knew this was where the coolest kids would be and when I got there, all the older kids were doing things that older kids do! Smoking weed, getting drunk, and partying. All of which I didn't know how to do.

At some point, the older brother made it known he was

rolling up a blunt.

As the big smoking circle began forming around the football star, I thought I had to be in it! This was my time to be cool and show my face with the coolest circle in school. I might as well be standing with the President!

I got my chance to hit the blunt twice, but I didn't feel "high" at all; I only felt "cool." Little did I know that was much better and pretty soon I was addicted to feeling cool, that is. (Feeling cool is a terrible gateway drug though, as it can lead to many other vices.)

And that was my first-time smoking weed.

Of course, I acted high when I went back inside and when the kid who was having the party came over and wanted to laugh about how "high we were," well, of course I did!

He must have seen me in the smoking circle! I knew that was a good move.

Inside, he pushed the microwave and made his own "BOOP" noise. I laughed hysterically and made my own "BOOOOOP" noise. I kept doing this over and over at his entertainment until I felt we had solidified our inside joke and he reminded me that he was the first one to get me "high!"

I now had an inside joke with the coolest dude from the other school!

Mission Accomplished.

I went from smoking weed every other weekend to every weekend. Then I went from smoking weed every other day to every day.

When I first started smoking weed, the psychoactive effects of the drug were much stronger on my mind, as my tolerances had not been built and chance would have it that a few years after "my first time smoking weed," I found myself back partying at the same house, the same way the older kids taught me. I had become good friends with MR. BOOP by this time and we were seniors partying now, and I went back to that same patio to smoke by myself...the same place where it all started in the first place. But this time something different happened. There was no big circle – it was just me – and the marijuana hit me hard psychoactive hard.

As I watched my friends through the windows from the back patio – through the looking glass, as you may say – I finally saw them for the first time.

After all these years, it was like that 7th grader again looking in on a group of people I didn't know. Except this time, I didn't want to be part of this group. I had been popular so long that I had become numb to the fakeness that surrounded me.

For some of these people, this was their first time being at that party. They so desperately wanted to be noticed by the "cool kids," or maybe even be friends with a person like me, that they always wore their Joker mask no matter how they felt inside. Always forcing their fake smiles and fake laughs just to fit in.

They needed that validation to be cool and I could see through their lies as they talked to one another. I watched them on mute, for the first time not hearing their bullshit. Through their façades.

Most of them only ever wanted to be friends with the "cool kids." Had it taken them four years to make it here?

All of them were so fake and forced in their friendships. I knew because I'd done my work years ago. This was the very place that I acted high and made dumbass "BOOP" noises just to fit in.

Now, I wondered which one of them was lying to fit in. None of them? All of them?

When I walked back inside, I heard a piercing "PHWWWWWHHHT- PHWOOOOOOH" coming from the kitchen and I really wasn't sure if this was the weed hitting me or if I was really hearing a whistle.

Then I heard it again..."PHWWWWWHHHT-PHWOOOOOOH." And when I turned the corner into the pantry, there were two freshmen holding a kettle and they were both laughing as they squeezed their lips together, making their own kettle sounds.

"PHWWWWWHHHT-PHWOOOOOOH," one said over and over as he tipped the kettle in his hand like he was pouring imaginary tea.

They looked over when I walked in and for a moment, I saw a young me in their sober eyes and I asked them, "Do you guys really wanna get high?" To which they quickly nodded yes.

"Then meet me on the back patio, I got this crazy shit from Guatemala...where the hills are just the right gradient and the soil has just enough acidity to produce the strongest weed in the world."

And if they wanted to meet me in back, I would smoke them out for free just like the seniors did for me when I was a freshman.

Of course, I lied. I waited till they left, and I rolled up some oregano I found in the kitchen. I even added some talcum powder just to "spice" it up a bit.

"This will send you to another dimension!" I told them out back, as I watched them hog down the blunt like fiends who hadn't smoked in years.

They couldn't smoke it fast enough as they passed it back and forth, puffing harder with each hit.

"Well done", I said.

"Wow, I'm really getting something," one said, coughing.

"This is WAY better than the other stuff", they both said, almost in unison, before one of them handed me the blunt.

I took a huge rip of my own and slowly blew the oregano smoke in their faces. With a big smile, I asked them, "Pretty cool, huh?"

First Time I Ate Shrooms

The first time I did magic mushrooms, I left a folded up note in my room the night before I left my parents' house, just in case anything happened to me and I wasn't normal afterwards.

It wasn't a suicide note...it was more like a 'death note,' in case I accidentally killed myself, or worse, fried my brain.

I was super afraid because "Magic Mushrooms" are a Schedule I drug, which is the worst class of drug you can take. Even above its buddies in the Schedule II class like Cocaine and Meth.

No, No, No! Magic Mushrooms stand alone with the drugs that can kill you on their first shot – no pun intended. That's right up there with the Ecstasies, the Acids and the Heroins of the world. That's my Schedule I advanced class, alright!

I only had one friend that had done them and could get them. This friend said we HAD to do them. He said he couldn't explain what it felt like, but if we liked smoking weed, we would love Shrooms! All he said to explain it was, "Shrooms are fuckin' crazy."

I wrote the death note because, on top of the anxiety, I had known about all the druggie urban legends.

The "Orange Juice" story was a favorite amongst trippers who really wanted to scare the newbies though. It was a story about a guy who "fried" himself so bad he permanently thought he was an orange and if anyone touched him, he would turn to orange juice.

He forever hopped around, a mindless carton of orange juice.

Pulp or No Pulp, I don't know.

Then there was the "It stays in your spine" story.

It had been said that the chemicals from these drugs stay in your spine forever and that once, a man who hadn't tripped in 20 years was sleeping with his wife one night when he rolled over and cracked his back.

The drug was released from his spine and he started to trip again. When he looked over at his wife, in the shadows of the night he saw the most hideous creature lying next to him! He was forever shaken and could never look at her the same again!

BUT! The legend that scared me most was a much more local story.

It was about a kid that my buddy knew, and they said he became different after taking the Shrooms...he was changed. No one could explain it and, slowly over time, he didn't want to talk to any of his friends anymore. I hoped this didn't become me.

Then the night came for the first time to do Shrooms and we threw caution to the wind. Four of us ended up blasted, sitting in front of my buddy's house on the street curb. We sat stupefied for six hours like fried vegetables baking under the street nightlight.

The funny thing about these kinds of drugs is that when you're on them, you LOOK like you're on those kinds of drugs!

As time passed, I had to touch my arm, which felt like it was floating away from me. Then I had to touch my leg, which felt like it was floating in the other direction. I felt like I was slowly breaking apart and floating away.

As I started to talk to my friends and explain to them what was happening, I had to touch my jaw to make sure it didn't float away too!

How could my jaw work so far away from my face, I wondered?

After that experience, I went looking for more Shrooms. I went from never eating Shrooms, to eating them every six months, to every month.

Then every other weekend to every weekend. Each trip taking my mind to a new place, each trip just as extreme and unexplainable as the last.

The magic of The Shroom is that it has a knack for wanting to bring up any buried emotion or unresolved thought or trauma that you try and hide. That is the first thing the Shroom will bring to your mind because secretly, it is always on your mind.

The first thing that always came to my mind: *I shouldn't take drugs.*

I could never wrap my head around the idea that what was made to seem like the most illicit drug of all was making me think "good" thoughts. Profound, as they say.

I didn't like my feelings or thoughts to be dismissed as a "drug" or being "fucked up." The Shroom kept me away from alcohol and pills and every other drug you could imagine (for most my life).

They opened my third eye and set me on a spiritual path.

Everything else was weak in comparison and I had no need for other drugs, and today science is proving Psilocybin to cure depression and alcoholism.

But you know what I noticed? None of the people that I took them with felt the same way. You had to be a little fucked up or run with the wrong crowd to want to take Shrooms...

They were dirty and "grown on cow shit." To most of my friends, it was just another drug. The experiences didn't mean anything to them. For them, it was just another way to get fucked up, just another way to escape reality and their problems for a night.

Over time I stopped talking to all these people, all my "friends" that I had nothing in common with. All we had in common was that we were stupid enough to take this drug together and I wanted nothing to do with these low-lifes anymore.

Then it hit me, about the stories I had heard, when I was afraid. About the kid who took Shrooms...and he was changed, because now it was a true story about me.

Bad Medicine

The Native Americans were the first people I ever heard say something could be "Good Medicine" or "Bad Medicine."

This seemed like an oxymoron that never made any sense to me. How could there be "Bad Medicine?" Wasn't all "Medicine" supposed to be good for you?

From all the stories we know from the Native Americans, we the Medicine Men and Women were pretty cool people. Everyone wanted to see them, and it seemed like they cared about the people they were giving the medicine to. They didn't make medicine for money.

Today, no one wants to see our doctors because our medicine men do it for money. Our doctors have no spirit in their medicine, no soul, no humanity! In fact, we tell our doctors if they want to be good at healing, they need to care less about their patients, they need to take their emotion out of it, to get the "job done." They might as well be mechanics fixing a car. American "pharmacists" and "doctors" look at us no different than a machine that can be fixed by changin' some fluids or replacing broken parts. They don't truly care about us or about givin' us that good medicine, as long as the companies can turn a buck on an average Joe.

If a person goes to the doctor, they HAVE to try and fix them, even if they think nothing's wrong. The mechanic can't say, "Come back in a week and maybe it will be fine!"

Even when we tell people that "side effects" may worsen, they still gobble it up and ask for more and the spiritless doctor doesn't care because if a new problem arises from the old Bad Medicine, the mechanic can fix that too! And hey, if they get any side effects, maybe they'll need some more pills for those too! They get a lot of money for fixing people and they can do this "healing" thing all day!

So, while we might think of Bad Medicine as putting leeches on some medieval peasant, I think we have a new, much more expensive Bad Medicine among us.

First Time I Did Morphine

I used to work at a joint called Chicken Shack. This one was a very...dysfunctional...establishment.

Once we used a 'gravity bong' in the chicken freezer and after I got stoned, I would look at the chicken and think how cruel it was for 10 chickens to die for an order of 20 wings. I guess you could say people really have no idea what goes on around their food, the animal killing...and the weed smoking.

I had a nice little gig managing the barbeque station and one time we had an order where the customer didn't want any BBQ sauce on their ribs. They wanted them "dry."

Well, they must have not known they were already sauced up and instead of making new ones, my manager told me to just wash the BBQ sauce off under the sink. A little tacky, but after a good washing and a few minutes back on the grill, they were as good as new!

My manager got fired a few years later for watching porn in the back office, by the way. I think the main reason though was that he had no concern for the customers' peanut allergies. The place was no longer a "NUT-FREE" establishment.

Anyways, there was this lady who worked there, a single mom with two younger daughters. She was a down-and-out type of the highest degree and, weirdly enough, she was always saying how she 'thought 'bout' me when touching herself in the shower' and I was only 16 at the time. She didn't give AF and one day she was talking about taking "Addys" (Adderall).

I never knew anything about them because I was never one to take pills. (I cried once when I saw my mom smoke a cigarette!)

Yet she insisted I take one – just "try it." She said they were "30 MG-ers" and it was similar to a drug they used to call Ritalin. Now Ritalin, I had heard of that before...it was what they gave the kids who tweaked in my class.

She sensed my nervousness and told me it wasn't a big deal – this is what she gave her daughters for their ADD and if they took it, then why should I be worried? And since she was in charge of the prescription, that means she would take them, sell them, or in this case...give them to me.

The first one I took, I felt it quick.

I was focused as I pulled and dropped chicken from the fryers, not even splashing a bit of boiling hot grease on my face or arms.

Immediately, I asked for more and the next one sent me into overdrive. I was buzzing like a beehive, working more diligently than I had ever before. I felt invincible and thought how cool this Adderall drug was.

Then I asked for one more, and she gave it up but said, "This is the last one."

After I took (x3) 30 MG-ers; I now insisted that I should be the one to stay and close work that night, and well, everyone else said it was a good idea too!

I cleaned that shithole spotless! I was like a superhuman, focused, not hungry, and alert! And I also didn't sleep a wink that night...

Fast-forward years later and I would meet Addy again because it was the 'collegiate wonder drug of choice.' From what I could tell, the students had learned of its superpowers and the doctors would give this Good Medicine to anyone who showed up to see their ugly faces. All you had to do was tell them you had a problem...NOW!

Addys were so available that taking them was the standard operating procedure and I would have days scheduled into my week where I planned to take an Addy. This was so I could "get shit done."

It didn't take someone long to think of snorting Addy and it wasn't much longer before I snorted one myself for the first time. My roommate (who had a script) was the first one I saw do it.

I never had a prescription personally, but those who did and took it every day became numb to the "limitless" effects and it became something they needed just to get level. Like any other addict, they had built up a tolerance and were always chasing that first high. Now they were taking Adderall just to feel normal. Now they needed it just to wake up and get out of bed. We would take little "bumps" at parties and I would quietly laugh at the idea that, unlike swallowing it and letting the Good Medicine take its course, snortin' it was a direct shot to the dome. After you snorted an Addy, instantly you would be awake and alert. Take enough and you would find that you couldn't get drunk and your dick wouldn't work. Then of course the only thing to bring you down from all the anxiety was to smoke some weed.

Then one semester, I started a new class where I was randomly seated next to a very skinny, quiet girl. She didn't talk much, but when she did, it was always just a whisper.

Everyone else said she had a slight lisp, but really, I just thought she was noticeably quiet.

For weeks she didn't say anything, but then one day, she started telling me about how her boyfriend got arrested the night before. The police kicked in the door and raided them for selling pills. She was nervous and erratic. I wasn't sure why she was telling me this. When the class met again in a few days, she didn't say much, other than she didn't like having a man 'not around.'

Again, I didn't think twice, but at the end of class she said, "Are you going to 'man up' or what!?"
I understood now.

Quickly I realized the reason she was so skinny is that she was a heavy pill popper herself. The first time we hung out, she asked me if I wanted any Vicodin and I didn't think much of it; I had taken it before if I had pain. Not something I did for fun, but if she was giving them to me for free, why not?

The more we hung out, the more I got free Vicodin from her.
Until one day she told me she had a different pill. This time it was something she called an "Oxy," short for Oxycontin.

Don't ask me why people don't call these drugs by their scientific names. I think maybe it sounds too nerdy. I had never taken Oxycontin and knew nothing about it. The only thing I DID know was that I used to hear rappers sing about it about having "OXYCOTTEN ALL IN THEIR VEINS."

This pill was a lot stronger and the effects numbed my whole body. Still, I didn't think twice. I would come home at 2am and smoke a blunt with my roommates who would laugh at how high I was. This would go on and on, always new, random pills. Always climbing the ladder with more Good Medicine I had never heard of when one day after class, I was standing in her kitchen and she asked me to grab two little pills, the likes of which I had never seen before. They were no bigger than a seed and, of the colorful assortment of painkillers we had taken, these were the smallest.

Then that fear hit me hard like I was going into the unknown like the first time I had done Shrooms. I started thinking about how I'd told myself I would never do this again.

"I should stop taking drugs!" always running in my mind.

I went with my gut on this one and I told her I didn't want to do it! You know at a party once, one of my friends gave me what he said was a Vicodin, but it was really a pill called "Suboxone." I was so drunk that I took him at his word, and the next thing I know, I was laid out flat on the ground. I couldn't even move, but my stomach was killing me. I came to find out that this is what they give to people who are withdrawing from heroin. Little did I know that Suboxone mixed with alcohol is a deadly little cocktail that can kill you, and all I can say is a little bit of good luck got me through that Bad Medicine.

I was surely not going to trust anyone anymore...I learned my lesson and that is when I heard a quiet whisper loudly say, "Come on, have I ever lied to you before?"

Her words faintly rolled out: "Jusssst try it, you'll be fine. I take it all the time, and if I can take it, then I promisssssssssssse nothing will happen to you."

And that was the second time I gave way to peer pressure. I was never pressured to smoke weed or drink. I wanted to do that, but pills were something that I knew wasn't right or to be taken for fun. I guess peer pressure from women is my weakness.

Of the little seedlike pill that was Morphine, I only agreed to take half of it. It was blue and had tiny little writing and I was amazed that people could put words on these petty things.

The effects of this pill, as expected, were strongest yet. It was a slow buildup to get here, and I guess, you could say, a long time coming.

Why and how did I end up taking more hardcore pills?

For such a small amount, I was shocked by how strong it was. Now I understood the war movies when the dying soldier is screaming out for "more Morphine!"

Shortly thereafter, I started to resent her – sure, she wanted a "real" relationship, but did she really think we could have a "real" relationship?

She thought this was real? Getting fucked up and being comfortably numb?

OHHH! How she knew nothing of me...did she really think I could wifey up a druggie like her? I wouldn't stick around any longer to find out what was lined up next.

After one semester and with a holiday break soon, I had decided I would break up with her right before then. I would be leaving campus for a few weeks and that would be a perfect escape.

I told her whatever it was that we had, whatever we called this, it was done, and I wouldn't be seeing her anymore. In her defense, she really wasn't that bad – a quiet girl with a habit. It was just that maybe I thought too highly of myself to be with someone who was really just like me.

Ironically, when I told her it was over, it turned out to be perfect timing, because she had something to tell me too!

She had an STD, and now...she said I had it.

FUCK! I thought. The timing reeks of revenge, but I've only known this girl barely a semester. Who knew what that prison bird before me could have given her? Maybe she had it all along and just now decided to tell me as her final breakup kill shot. This was the kind of thing that couldn't be ignored.

The last thing I ever heard from her was a slithering "Sssssssssorrrry" as she hung up the phone.

The thought of having this STD ate away at my mind until I could make it into the doctor's office, but since I was too cowardly to see the local family doctor and face that shame during vacation, I waited a long two weeks until I made it back to school to see a campus doctor.

The treatment/ testing was super cheap on campus I guess they did not want STDs to spread...

On the way to the doctor's office, I chugged as much water as I could. I wanted to just get it over with. I couldn't wait to get there, take the piss, and be done with it. The anxiety was making me so woozy that when the doctor called me back, I was ready to piss my pants. I asked him if we could please just hurry because I had just slammed a bunch of water on the way over to see him and I was ready to pee now!

A creepy old grin slowly grew across his face and he let out a deep bellowing laugh that filled the stale medical room as he slapped on his blue rubber latex gloves and said, "This isn't a urine test, Son."

"This is a swab test."

In his hand he held a giant Qtip and explained how he would have to stick that into my pee hole just to be sure.

My heart sank – she got me.
The pain of a giant Qtip being stuck up your pee hole is quite excruciating.

let.me.tell.you.

You see, she didn't think the breakup was fair or justified and she wasn't just going to let me enter and exit her ecosystem so easily.

She wanted to make sure she made an imprint on me like I did on her, something that I would never forget, and she did.

When it was all said and done, I was as clean as a whistle, but I had a terribly similar thought about my friends and the people I was getting involved with, and that was...I should probably stop doing drugs.

Puppy Love

When we were younger and had a crush on someone, what did all the "grown-ups" say?

"Aww, it's just puppy love."

They called it "puppy love," but what they meant was: "immature, not grown yet, not real love." What could children ever know about love? It's puppy love! When you get older, you'll understand!

No one questions the fact that a child can love a neighbor, teacher, mother, father, sister, or any other person or animal you can imagine. But when it comes to a child loving another child, we are quick to dismiss that love. Aren't the greatest love stories ever told of soul mates who met when they were children? Our society now destroys these starcrossed relationships before they even start.

81

People's minds are so deep in the gutter, it's hard for older creeps to imagine a love not based on sex. They have the worst thoughts on their own minds all the time that it's hard for them to see anything other than through a dark paradigm.

When we see innocent love, not built around sex, well, then we dismiss it!

Then right around the age of 16, people start finding out that they feel "love" again. We are told anything before that is just puppy love. Society's so obsessed with sex that without it, love isn't real.

Laws are made and we are taught that sex is love. Then at 16, we can have sex with others the same age as us.

Then, the first person we have sex with becomes our "first love."

BUT! For the second time in your life, you will be doubted, and your relationship will be labelled "not real." They will then call you High School Sweethearts.

Even if these "Sweethearts" have sex and "feelings" like adults do, these get dismissed too. They don't pay bills! They don't work! They don't know anything! What is their love? That love which hasn't faced loss, adultery, or hardship.

And once again, love is redefined and doubted. So, loving someone gets very confusing.

My whole life, I've been told "what love is" and "what it isn't." And love isn't High School Sweethearts.

I was never taught to hold onto anyone for life. I was always taught there's "plenty of fish in the sea." Always letting more fish into my ecosystem, always comparing each fish to the last.

So, we say...what do High School Sweethearts know about love?

"No one in high school stays together."

The "wise elders" think that if it didn't work for them, it won't work for you – so they continue to teach their adulterous ways.

I call it Serial Monogamy.

Now, heading into your 20s, you've had love without sex and sex without love, and you're never told which one's right or wrong, never even told there was a difference.

The Serial Monogamist always thinks relationships have an expiration date: six months or until someone stops having fun. At first, they are renewed and have dreams of marriage until the "honeymoon" phase ends and the fireworks slow down and crushes become more frequent.

We start to wonder what we're doing with this person.
There's plenty of fish in the sea...Tinder makes you only one swipe away from getting that new fish! We start to think about how many relationships we've wasted...what's one more? So, we go out and cheat - we find that fire and passion in someone else and we feel good again, our Cold Heart found "love" again.

The Guts

Call me crazy...but I suspect there's a secret alien invasion happening here on Earth, right under our noses. Okay, not literally under our noses. Not enough space. But the point is this, the invasion's happening. And we're none the wiser.

An invasion of the "body snatchers," if you will. I call these alien invaders..."The Guts."

The Guts are parasitic, they set up shop in your abdomen like a worm or other parasite. Then they grow (depending on how much you eat.) And to help them grow as much as possible, they need to make sure you eat enough. So, they hatched a plan. A plan to grow.

Without using overt force, unlike most invasions, The Guts did something very clever. They introduced a 'new word' into our Earth languages (sadly, something I could not do!)

The word "hangry."
That feeling when you're angry due to being hungry.

The desire to eat that makes our tempers monstrous. Intolerable.

And this desire to eat would be kept at the forefront of our brains, so the Guts schemed, due to this new word.

Appropriately, living rent free on the tip of our tongues. And so, we'd be encouraged to eat more and thereby ensure the Guts were always well fed, and able to grow.

And isn't it funny during alllllll those years before "Hangry" was invented, and for alllllll those people on the planet during that time, not one of them had ever known this feeling before? I mean...we didn't even have a word for it!!!

So, when "Hangry" hit mainstream, that's when I knew the Guts were taking control. And as they invaded more and more bodies, more and more people became hangrier and hangrier.

When I was little, people used to say, "Trust your gut feeling," but now I've come to fear the Guts and any of their "feelings." They have taken over completely, and we need to be remorseless in their ejection!

Once the Gut mind is in charge and has taken over the brain, there's no telling how much damage could be done! This is when they're at the helm, pulling the strings.

And what's the main goal of these secret invaders? To eat and to shit! Both of which feel good to the Gut.

Then, once the Gut has placed a host body in a systematic state of shitting and eating, only then can the Gut live happily, growing larger and larger every day.

Eating more and more.
Shitting more and more.
Growing Hangrier and Hangrier.

The scary part is there's no telling how large it can grow! On television sometimes, I see crazy Guts that have grown so large their host body can no longer move. Six-hundred-pound people are stuck in their own beds! The casualties are rising in this war!

Sadly, there's only one way to get rid of this alien infestation, and that is to Kill the Gut!

To defeat the Gut, you've gotta beat it at its own game. Eat healthy and exercise regularly! Trim that Gut down! Cut it down to size! We're waging a war, repelling an invasion! Not with guns and tanks, but with low-calorie smoothies and spin classes! Uncle Sam Needs You to lose 50 pounds! The fate of the nation depends on it.

No Imagination

We forget that as kids, we loved coloring, drawing, and creating. Some of us created havoc. Some of us created friendships. We all created memories. As children, we had this need to create and express ourselves in whichever way possible, and sometimes that meant carving your name into your desk or writing all over Mom's walls! The school curriculum and our parents (who were the smart "adults") collectively decided that each year we should be FORCED to go to school with colored pencils and cotton balls for creating. We headed out with a toolbox of artsy-craftsy materials to glue together armies of popsicle Frankensteins that only our mothers could love.

Then as we got older, we stopped expressing ourselves. We did more but we felt less, whereas a child does less but feels more. *Do you not remember how big a deal it was to color inside the lines?*

It seems all the kids' movies and children's fairy tales have turned out to be true: adults have lost their imaginations! What used to be exciting brainstorms turned into tiny drops of rain. Today people imagine things like "a day without coffee."

Human beings not only have the ability of SIGHT, but also VISION.

SIGHT is what you objectively see right in front of your eyes, but VISION is the ability to see into the future! *"To envision, to IMAGINE a better life."*

Why don't you ever see adults playing in the snow?

Because the adult can't see the snow for anything other than what is right before their eyes: droplets of frozen water. What is in their SIGHT.

To those with no imagination, the snow has no more meaning. It is a burden that gets in our way and stops us from doing more.

For a child, the snow can be anything they ENVISION, anything they imagine! A snowman, a snow fort, a snowball, a snow angel.

The child sees unlimited potential in the world around them, through their imagination. The child sees the truth of our world for what it really is, and what it could be.

Remember what you knew as a child, because the universe never changed we did. The Universe contains unlimited potential and through your imagination, you can give meaning and life to that potential, something that no one else can.

True Evil

In films the "bad" guy is always obvious. They're evil-looking: a scar down the cheek, holding a knife, banging a door, wearing menacing features, in dark clothing, shooting a harsh expression. These are the signs, and the list goes on.

BUT! True Evil, like serial killers, will look you dead in the eye and smile as they drive by going to church on Sunday morning.

In films, books and on TV, the audience has no doubt who the VILLAIN is. But in real life, things aren't so simple. The villain wears a grin, they're charming, they make us feel at ease, they're relaxed, they make us feel at home. Lulling the victim into a false sense of security.

In real life, **the victims wear the scars, not the villains.**

The manipulative and abusive partner who waves at the neighbors before going into his home to beat his wife. What about the guy in the alley, who asks for a smoke knowing that if he seems friendly, you'll let him close? Or the salesman, gleeful, complimentary, and charming as he cons an old lady out of her savings.

They behave this way because they have to, to survive.

Anything else and they'd be found out. It's natural selection for crooks. The Origin of Deviants.

For true evil to survive, it must go unnoticed, under the radar. The crooks who are able to 'keep up appearances' are the ones who survive longest without getting caught. The ones who wear evil on their sleeve quickly get found out, and wind up in jail. Consequently, the surviving crooks, the ones on our streets, those are the ones with veneers of normality: the kind of personas, charming smiles. The ones that make you think: *Hey, he's someone I can trust.*

This position of trust helps them even further with their evil intentions: from this position they can more easily manipulate, cheat, and harm their way through life, taking advantage of those around them.

I've learnt to be suspicious of someone with 'too big of a smile,' an unsettling level of charm, teetering on the edge of "over the top." And, even more, I don't 'write off' those who wear a tough expression, those who don't care if you think they aren't nice. Often, they're the sweetest cookies in the end, 'cos they've got a reason to look tough: they've been through shit.
Don't judge a book by its cover, as they say.

—

And so most people these days "play" bad, but if we were to

talk about really doing something bad, they couldn't do it. The nonbelievers find it fun to dress up as the Devil or as other evil things, but if I were to talk about digging up a grave to make a quick buck on some dead person's jewelry, well, then I couldn't find a handful for those sorts. They treat "evil" and "bad" like movie characters, something that is simply trivial and "made up."

That's because most people are fortunate enough to never encounter the true evil that exists in this world. To encounter true evil means to be afflicted, for life!

If you were unfortunate enough to be raped or kidnapped, or if your daddy is a serial killer - these things never leave you.

True evil leaves a permanent imprint on the people it touches. The acts they are victims of, haunt them for life. That's its defining feature. Its calling card.

On TV, I have seen the victims of these evil people and some of them are so ashamed to talk about their story that the station blacks out their faces and changes their voice! Now that is some true evil: making you carry shame for something YOU didn't even do – for your whole life.

Today so many people are taken advantage of because they think the 'bad guy' is going to show up with a knife in hand, or huge evil eyes that glow in the night, or other big warning signs. They never stop to realize that the people who smile right to your face are sometimes the ones that want to see you bleed the most.

Extra Ice

Every time I hear someone ask for "extra ice" in their drink, a little bit of me dies inside.

Do they NOT know what alchemy had to happen to produce 'hard water!'

Imagine the poor souls that died wishing for a drop of water...and you want "extra ice?" The audacity!

But you know what?
If you can't beat 'em, join 'em.

Now, when I go to McDonald's or some other fast-food joint to get my combo number six, I get water...with "extra ice!" Other lowly often freak out and say something like... "YOU GOT WATER...BUT YOU PAID FOR POP WITH THAT COMBO!"

To which I chuckle with my two pound cup of ice and think, *No, I didn't...I paid for the ice and I'm gonna get my money's worth.*

(My friend Dolla, he asks for a second cup "just for ice.") *He really gets his money's worth!*

Strangely enough, I'm starting to think that other low-lows don't even know what they're paying for anymore.

They tell me I should get the soda pop because water is free, but if I ask for a bottle of water, then it will cost me more. How can it cost me more to upgrade to a water bottle...if the water is free?

DAMNIT! It's all so confusing that I figure I'll just pay for the ice.

Imagine all that had to happen to bring me this "hard water." From the electricity to power the freezer, to the nuts and bolts of the metal ice machine... Extra ice...now that's money well spent.

But the best part of it is, when I'm on my way home, and all that's left in the cup is the extra ice...you wanna know what I do?

I throw it out the window!

What else am I supposed to do with all that extra ice they gave me?

Power of Zero (Part 1)

I love to piss math people off by telling them: **I don't believe in the number zero.**

I say, look around the room...point to zero.

Or better yet, put zero of something into your hand. You can't do it.

In math, I was taught that anything multiplied by zero equals zero. But if I pick something up, hold it in my hand, then multiply that object by zero in my mind...it's still there.

But, if I did it on a calculator, it would show me zero.

I can multiply it by two in my mind and visualize another. Or I can multiply it by ten and see much more. I can even deduct one and put it down, but I can't make it disappear. I cannot

94

make something become nothing.

In the same way that a black hole is all consuming, it's not a planet, yet it sits amongst the rest of countable space.

Zero is the absence of a number, a black hole, the absence of a planet. Calling zero a number would be the same as calling a black hole a planet!

And that's why I don't really believe in this number zero thing: it just doesn't seem to work in reality! And what's more important, mathematical theory or reality?

I'm no mathematician, but I do know a mathematical truth about zero which no one has taught us... Zero is ALL consuming!

Mathematically, when ZERO is associated with other numbers, it swallows them into its nothingness!!

The Power of Zero affects our minds in the same way: a black hole that consumes all our thoughts around it, into its nothingness!

Often, I hear people say things like they have "zero abilities" or "zero talent," "zero friends, zero fun, zero money." They constantly see themselves in this empty state of zero, instead of seeing what we DO have.

We love ZERO so much that companies now litter their deals with promises of zero:

ZERO CALORIES, ZERO INTEREST, ZERO MONTHLY PAYMENTS, and my favorite...ZERO CASH DOWN!

Maybe we love its emptiness, capturing both everything and nothing together in a mysterious promise of endless possibilities.

Maybe it appeals to the gaps in our soul. I say ZERO is not a real place, only a place holder, and you can't be in a place that isn't real! I just focus on the real ones, or as they used to say...count your blessings!

Power of Zero (Part 2)

I heard that people in Japan aren't told when they're going to be executed. I mean, people in Japan *who are on death* row aren't told when they're going to be executed. Not just all people in Japan.

Although, actually, it's true of the average Japanese person too: they aren't told the day they'll be executed but that's just because they're not scheduled for such a grizzly fate...

Anyway, digression aside, the news of their death only reaches them when they actually receive the fatal shot, zap, or stick.

Not knowing when the end's coming, but knowing it's coming all the same would likely make every minute torture. It could be the next second, or the next. Or this one. Or that one. Ooh, that's no way to live!

Anyway, this is what they do, I'm just informing you!

And...this is what I call putting the "Zero Up Front." And...most people live their life like this.

Waking up each and every day without knowing what is going to come. If death were only a few hours away, most of them really didn't take the time to notice it.

And so, when people don't know the end date of something, they approach it like you would a treadmill: always thinking about how far they have gone from their starting point of zero. Not how much left they've got out in front of them. Thus, the "Zero Up Front."

So, those who put the "Zero Up Front" will constantly focus on how far they have come from the start, instead of how much closer they are to the end. People hate running because each step is a dread when you start thinking about how many steps you have taken from the start, from that zero up front. Why would anyone keep going? BUT if you put the "Zero on The End," the way you look at something becomes vastly different.

If the doctors tell someone they only have so much time to live, or you know your vacation on the beach is coming to an end, or people know the day they're going to die, as on death row in the United States, then that is what I call putting the "Zero on The End."

When you have a point where you know something ends, it changes everything about your experience up until that point.

Sadly, some people even put the "Zero on The End" of a relationship and even though they can't quite pin the exact date, they know it's coming to an end in their heart and mind.

98

When people know the end date of something, when they see the "Zero at The End," they approach all that time leading up to it differently. *Does your clock count up or does it count down?*

Sometimes athletes get a second wind and reenergized when they know there are only a "few minutes left on the clock." Or a good marathon runner will set their pace so they finish strong. Sometimes people make a bucket list and sometimes people have a midlife crisis.

Imagine if I did a 'five-finger death punch' on you and you could only walk five more steps before your heart exploded out of your chest and bled out – don't you think each step would be the most important one of your life?

Life is not about how many steps you have taken, it's about how many steps you've got left, and because of that, each step becomes that much more valuable.

Like a roll of toilet paper, it's not until you're at your last few sheets that you realize you took the first wad for granted!

When you consider every step could quite literally be your last, thousands of steps become easy.

For most of us, it's only after a doctor places an expiration date on us or puts our "Zero at The End" - that we take the time to appreciate our limited time here on Earth. When you put the "Zero on The End" and realize that the end is much nearer than it appears, then you realize each day is not a dread connected to the one before it. Each day is more valuable than the last, and the closer we get to our inevitable end, the more important each moment becomes.

99

Power of Zero (Part 3)
The Curse of the Libra

I think it's fair to say the only thing better than one zero is, well, two zeroes.

Naturally, one could say that triple zeroes are better, maybe even quadruple zeroes, but I would argue that double zeroes are really the sweet spot.

In fact, anything more than double zeroes seems to get a little bit confusing – you know how they say the next closest galaxy is 236,000,000,000,000,000 km away from Earth… yeah, the whole thing just gets a little silly after about seven of them.

Or at least for my American mind, because how lucky our money only has two zeroes. Imagine if I had to deal with currencies like the Vietnamese Dong or Indonesian Rupiah where their money has six zeroes on it. How confusing!

I'll take my 1 American dollar with no zeroes - over their 100,000 Rupiah any day!

And so, it took me years of working with aerospace engineers to really understand that some people really love double zeroes, or what they call "100%." They obsessed over it and would spend all their days getting there.

100% has become one of our favorite numbers, but, I say, 100% is a weak number and a bad system of measurement!

To better understand this, consider that NBA superstar Steph Curry made 105 three-pointers in a row.

Now, if you were to simply measure him out of the traditional 100% or 100 shots, you would not actually get a true representation of how good he is. You need a better, more robust system of measurement to capture his abilities. *You need more zeroes!*

Now, if you measure him out of 1,000 shots, you will have a much better understanding of good he really was. The only time we measure in thousandths is when a realtor wants to sell me a house I can't afford. *(Only a "few hundred thousand" they say!)*

Now, if you measure him out of 10,000 shots, you will really know how good he was. If he made just one, that would be one ten thousandths. This is the standard unit of measurement in High Precision Engineering – one ten thousandths and/or four places to the right of the decimal (.0001).

Today, most of society has very weak systems of measurment or you could say, we don't use enough zeroes! Whether is be 100% or 50/50 or 1 year.

Maybe it's the Sun, or maybe it is grade school, but most people threw out the entire year of 2020 – **THE WHOLE YEAR**! What happened to making every minute count? *Talk about throwing the baby out with the bathwater!*

Even a child would tell you that they are not simply just seven or eight; rather, seven and a half or eight and three-quarters.

Even a child understands how weak measuring by one year is.

What I've come to know as the curse of the Libra is that for the Libra to be in balance, they have to be 50/50.

Libras try to split our differentials and balance our zeroes out, but sometimes you have to tip the scales and go all in. Sometimes you have to stack your zeroes and put them all on one side of the equation.

Sometimes you have to give a 100 and that means some things you gave 50 to will now get 0.

Other things you gave 50 to will now get 100.

Not 50/50 rather 100/0 <--- *And now look, you have already gained another zero! Good for you!*

Tip the scales, go all in!

Many share the Curse of the Libra in their relationships

when they say a relationship is 50/50.

50/50 <--- *Only one zero on each side of the equation. Ha! Just one ZERO!! What are we, cavemen here?*

What would relationships look like if we measured with more zeroes?

Instead of 50/50, what if we said 100/100 or what if we went 10,000/10,000?

What do you think those relationships would look like?

Power of Zero (Part 4)

I had a teacher once – for the sake of this story, I'll call him the Professor. He was an older gent and taught one of them...'science classes.' It was a tough class made up of two parts: lab and lecture.

Now, the class itself only had a few hundred points over the whole semester. This meant that every quiz, exam, and assignment was crucial because each time you missed a question, your whole grade dropped lower.

In the lab, we were always doing demonstrations, and I noticed the Professor had a knack for calling up the prettiest girls to do the demonstrations and show the rest of the class what to do. He never called a guy, or an unattractive girl, and to me, it was obvious what he was doing. In his defense, I did pay great attention during those demonstrations.

After some time, my conspiracy about his affinity for the pretty girls turned out to be true. I'm not sure why - maybe he saw a little bit of himself in me. Whatever the case may be, I ended up befriending the Professor. He'd always remind me about how beautiful his students were. Every so often he would drop the classic line: "If I was 40 years younger...I would love to take these beautiful ladies out."

From then on, me and the Professor had a common understanding.

With time, this meant that every lab became an inside joke about the girls, and our admiration of their beauty.

It wasn't quite as it sounds. The Professor genuinely thought his students were pretty, not in a "creepy" way but more like an "old man admiring beautiful birds in the forest" kind of way, knowing he could never catch one.

Anyways, to cut to the chase...I failed every lab and lecture quiz that semester.

Like most of the other students on a failing ship, I calculated what my final chance to pass was and my calculations told me that for the final exam, I needed 93% not to flunk!

It was no question that a 93% on the final exam of this caliber would be a feat I had never achieved in my entire collegiate career.

But now, I had to do it in one of the hardest classes I'd ever taken. I was beaten before the fight.

As predicted, I didn't pass or get my 93%, I bombed the test and failed the course.

A few weeks later though my grades came back, and I went online to see what the final damage really was, and to my surprise, I had a B+!

Incredible, I thought. It was one of my best grades that semester! A big, beautiful B+ looking me square in the eye, as real as could be. Right away I knew it was a mistake though, it was impossible...

I failed everything in that class. I don't even think I passed one of the quizzes. It was quite impossible for me to pass...so what happened?

Of course, I wasn't going to question it, but I did wonder how it happened and when I went back and looked at all my grades, it took me the longest time to find what happened, but I did find it...

The Professor had, as we called it, "fat fingered" one of my assignment grades.

One of my quiz scores from the lecture was a **100/10.**

I had 100 points on a 10-point assignment.

Well, needless to say that the extra 90 points boosted my grade unbelievably and that one extra zero changed the entire course of my life.

Talk about the power of zero, wow!

And while I could never prove what he did, I knew in my heart he helped me out there. The one extra zero was such an easily deniable mistake if I was stupid enough to squeal on him.

I never saw the Professor again, but he certainly did not let his comrade down. The Professor taught me that there is no "one way" for anything in life. There's always a way "outside of the box."

Even on something as strict as a college class, which I had been led to believe could only be passed one way. I now understood that people control all numbers and people alone give value to them.

The numbers didn't mean anything in themselves when I was in cahoots with the person creating them. It's a lot easier to get a raise when your dad's the boss!

In life, people will try and approach a problem like we do a class – one way – but rarely is there only one way. The old-timers used to say, "There's a million ways to skin a cat."

This is why we hate teacher's pet, because they don't get graded like the rest of us, and deep down in our hearts, we know all that brown-nosing pays off!

So, from then on, I stopped focusing on numbers and zeroes and started focusing on people.

Magical Items

I like to call my guitar a Magical Item.

My guitar or Magical Item has the ability to have great effects on the people around us. The secret is any object can become magically imbued with the human spirit. Through how we use objects, they can become greater than the sum of their individual parts.

A basketball, haircutting scissors, an oven, a bicycle, a telephone, a mirror, and even a chair. Any object that changes a person beyond a normal one is what I like to consider magical.

The guitar is my most Magical Item because I have spent so much time with it. (If you don't know what your most Magical Item is, ask an ex-lover to tell you what item of yours they would have destroyed first in the name of revenge!)

As for the guitar, I've put my spirit into it, so to speak. But for such a strong magical item like a guitar, there's a great amount of struggle that comes before you can wield it. My guitar has made me friends, impressed the ladies, and put me at the center of attention. It has also created jealousy and competition. I know, I know, I hate the guy that busts out the guitar at the party too.

A basketball in the hands of Michael Jordan changed the world. A computer in the hands of Bill Gates changed all of humanity. These were their Magical Items. (A basketball was not just a ball when being tossed around by MJ.)

Magical Items are all around us. When people pass away, any item of theirs becomes priceless to family members. If you're a famous person, your Magical Items may even get auctioned off for big money after you die! And you don't even have to be dead either because I heard one of those old sweaty pairs of shoes belonging to Michael Jordan went for half a million dollars in some fancy auction!

$250,000 for each shoe!!

For my guitar though, I knew that with such a powerful item, it would demand the utmost respect and training.

Excalibur surely wasn't mastered in a day!

That is the power of a Magical Item, to drive you and change you. To make you believe. I smile thinking that out there somewhere, there's a grandma baking up an old family recipe only she knows.

And so, she alone, with that oven and a tray of traditional chocolate chip cookies, could gain the favor of the world – now that's magic!

And it was all magical until one day I met someone who didn't agree with all this. He was a Buddhist monk who told me he'd renounced all his possessions, all his "Magical Items." He said he didn't believe in "material possessions" at all anymore. Lost them in a fire, he said.

This stumped me for a moment, and I asked him, "So you don't have ANY Magical Items?"

"No Magical Items here," he said, but apparently, he had never felt happier now that they were gone.

"Okay then, what would your exgirlfriend have the most pleasure in destroying after you broke up?" I asked him with confidence.

He thought for a moment, looking a little dumbfounded. Then said, "Probably my crack pipe..." My mouth fell open as a few seconds passed. "Just kidding," he said, laughing. "But FYI, we monks don't do 'girlfriends.'" Right, of course, I thought. He must have been listening to at least of some of what I told him because he then said, "Anyways, I've gotta go, have fun wanking over your guitar!"

I never saw him again.

Cold Hearted

One of the biggest lies that I believed when I was younger was that guys needed to "get bitches" to be "cool."

For a long time, I believed this to be true. I needed a woman to validate me more specifically, a pretty woman. So I allowed any "pretty woman" to enter my ecosystem, without ever considering that I didn't need to.

Sometimes an apple can be pretty on the outside, but it's not until you bite into it that you realize how rotten it is inside. Then, before you know it, you are in a toxic relationship - eating shitty apples.

Saying things and doing things you may have never done. Then there is the baby in the baby carriage and the divorce is on the way. *I've seen it a million times.*

Like a computer that has no protection and is vulnerable to viruses, if you let the wrong person into your life, there is no telling how much damage can be done to your ecosystem and there is no amount of validation that can make up for how much of your eco system they can destroy. It only takes one missile to sink your whole ship and be compromised financially, spiritually, and mentally.

Welcome to the ruins.

If I could go back in time and tell myself one thing, it would be, "DONT WORRY ABOUT HER, BRO."

Have you ever seen this funny movie about a 40yearold male virgin? It's called *The 40-Year-Old Virgin.* It's a comedy! That's funny! Someone who hasn't had sex. Wait. Why is that so funny?

Today men are taught they should sleep with anything that walks. Each woman a victory, a conquest, a notch on the old belt to further validate his toxic masculinity.

If you don't get any notches, you're a joke!

Those who are constantly going in and out of relationships getting notches, using others for validations, these are the ones who become cold-hearted, and you do not want them in your ecosystem. Like all things cold, when they touch you, they will make you a little bit colder too.

We're constantly 'shopping around' thinking about the better relationship we could have rather than working on what we do have. Our consumer culture mantra is leaking out of the shopping center and into the way we choose relationships, always looking for the next model to bring excitement.

The cold-hearted stop believing their relationships will last and they say things like "No one can love me."

They stop seeing the beauty in everyone's ecosystem; rather, they start scheming about what they can come in and take and there is no limit on what they will take. They assume love from other people is how their cold heart feels it: ingenuine, not real, fake, and selfish. They have hurt themselves and others over and over until they have no heart left to give anymore. Then breaking up with someone or screwing someone over is just another normal day. But we are not machines; we are not immune to the actions of others (as we like to think we are). All people leave a little bit of their heart and soul with whoever enters our life. When we act as a machine, cold and without heart, we find ourselves alone and depressed.

All love, all hate, all people leave an everlasting imprint on us, a footprint on our ecosystem.

Snozzberries

Of all the homemade cookin' I've had and restaurants I have been to, I've never ever had homemade "SODA POP."

So, I've been wondering: who is really behind this POP stuff? I never had Grandma's homemade "MOUNTAIN DEW" or Grandpa's secret "RED BULL" recipe. Personally, I think this is one of them conspiracy theories, because I don't think it's your local bakers making all this "POP" stuff!

Ohhhhhh no, this goes much deeper than the local baker, and trust me, I have run into some clever bakers...

I've never known a person in all my time that could pull off the special effects that these foods have nowadays.
You ever see a shaken-up Pepsi explode like a hand grenade in the hot summer heat? How about a little Mentos-- Coke improvised explosive device? Not a bad little experiment

to show the science class kiddies, eh?

I really thought about the whole periodic table of elements and what are the chances that a lowly cook could correctly mix all the salts and carbonation and sugars and caffeine that is needed for that POP we all know and love? Heck, it might as well be a secret recipe hidden behind a vault somewhere!
cough Coca-Cola *cough*

Now, good ole' fashioned American foods like chocolate milk and milk chocolate are clear about what they taste like, but what exactly did "Coca-Cola" or "Pepsi" taste like?

No one could really explain it to me...they just tasted like whatever they named it. Weird thing is they had commercials that always showed people who could tell the difference between them!

What did they taste like? Well...
The Pepsi tastes like Pepsi, and the Coke taste like Coke!
My GOD!
Willy Wonka was a true story!

The Snozzberries taste like Snozzberries!

Pecan Pie, Banana Splits, Orange Juice, Lemon Tarts, Grape Soda, Peanut Butter, Almond Joys, Apple Sauce, Ginger Ale, Strawberry Shortcake, Butter Beer, Cherry Syrup, Blueberry Muffins, and my favorite, Cinnamon Toast Crunch!
Woaahhhh, even worse than I originally suspected: we are not just dealing with a normal Willy Wonka. Instead, we've got some sick, twisted Willy Wonka from a parallel universe! Who, with his partner Slugworths over at FOOD CORP, like to hide their wacky foods behind what seem like naturally grown foods. If they called it what it really was, well, then you would never

buy it!

Sure, you have heard of Aspartame, but have you heard of 4-methylimidazole?

Where do you expect your local bakers to get these chemicals and secret ingredients listed on these food labels? Where do you expect them to get the Nitrogen to fill the bags of chips? It seems to me like you would have to be a wacky chemist of sorts to get these chemicals, doesn't it?

I guess, since no one really knows what's in any of our food anymore...fuck it! Might as well throw in Wonka's old boot for some extra flavor; in fact, I've already written a note to Bettermaid and requested a special flavor: Extra Nitro!

Three P Party

So, Willy and the Guts did a nice little number on all of America. They turned the whole country into sugar-loving maniacs...just like the story!

Wonka's key was this little white powder that's responsible for over 25,000 deaths a year in the US. Nope, not cocaine. The other one: sugar. But hey, at least cocaine doesn't rot your teeth. Old Wonka himself had to choose between cocaine and sugar, and he went with sugar - imagine that!

And with this army of sugar lovers came the addiction.

The lowly addicts are hooked on sugar without even knowing it and like any other addict, they ride the same rollercoaster of emotions: going up and down, feeling high then low, and always needing more and more to get level and feel "normal." Always thinking about the next snack or next "treat" to help us through the day, but hey, we 'earned it.'

I know now that when I eat a lot of sugar, I wake up depressed and I could never understand why I felt that way other than the fact it always happened after eating lots of sugar! I wonder who else is experiencing this? None the wiser of the sweet cause.

My bet is that there are a lot of people who have these same side effects of the 'Snozzberries' but instead, they think it is something else, maybe that depression. Truth is, Willy Wonka got us addicted in the womb! Willy Wonka and the Guts had a plan to get me addicted before I could even talk! From the time I was a baby, my mom was feeding me sugar in the womb because chances are, she was hooked on the cube too!

The tragedy is they get you hooked on the stuff while you're still young, so it wasn't a calculated effort for me to be 'addicted' but more a tragic, involuntary indoctrination, when you're too young to know better.

And by the time I became a little 'shithead kid' I was ready for my ritual "Three P Parties."

Pizza, Pop, and Parents.

Parents let the kids have so much sugar that sometimes the poor little creatures end up rejecting the drug and they throw up everywhere! But of course, none of the other parents think to stop the madness…not even when little Billy is projectile vomiting rainbow cake all over Karen's couch!

No, no, no! The Three P Parties go on for years and years, and more and more kids join in. And so, from our early years we are taught sugar is fun. In fact, I can't remember the last time I had fun without having a little sweet treat to go with it! Bowling alleys, arcades, theme parks, stadiums, anywhere we go for fun, there's a light dusting of sugar to go with it. A little bit of ice cream, a little bit of candy, and a lot of pop and snozzberries hiding behind every counter.

From a parent's perspective, sugar is an easy tool that can be used to control kids. "DO this and you'll get a treat." "Don't do that or you'll lose your candy, little Billy!" Ironically, giving the kid a treat ramps up the 'hyperactive behavior' that the bribe was supposed to suppress!

Be a good boy and you'll get some candy...oh SHIT, now you're now acting up – bad boy! It's a vicious cycle, because as the parent becomes more frustrated by the child's sugar-induced frenzy, the parent pleads even more and more fervently for them to behave, using the very chemical responsible as further motivation. A vicious ring...a ring doughnut glazed in sugar.

Monkey See – Monkey Do

They say that the best way to learn is not from your own mistakes, but by watching others' mistakes. It's called Vicarious Learning. This way you don't have to make the mistakes for yourself and suffer the negative consequences. You can just skip right to the good stuff. That is, unless you are one of 'em sadists who PREFERS to learn the hard way, of course.

So, I thought, what better way to learn from the mistakes of others than watch all the old people before me? Each one surely taking a shot at their ways.

The druggies never last long, the lazy ones are always depressed, the workers are always stressed - but the old people, now they've got it figured out!

These old monkeys made it against all the odds, and they have seen all the ways of all the people before them.

Isn't this why we always want to ask super old people: what exactly is the trick to being so old? What is the secret that you learned along the way that helped you make it through this fuss we call life?

One thing is for sure, they seem to always be dressed for the occasion! They wear comfortable shoes and warm hats and they may even overdress just to head the grocery store. But what have they learned over time? The importance of clothing and how it reflects your character. Dressing nice is a show of respect for other people. After all, they are the ones that must look at you!

And hey, when you get that old, that may be what you die in!

And so, how often do you see young people unkempt or dressed sloppily – us millennials couldn't care less for how others view us. Hey! If you don't like the way I look, then that's a problem with YOU, not me.

Was it not Mark Zuckerberg, the millennial genius of Facebook himself, who showed us we could attend high-profile meetings and run the world - in a hoodie! Funny thing is, years later, I saw this Zoidberg guy in front of the Senate being asked about Facebook and you know what?
He was in a suit!

HA! The suits get everyone in the end!

The second thing I have learned is that even though old people seem to be moving slow, they are always on time!

Like the tortoise and the hare. Us younger people and the average person is so busy buzzing around trying to do so many things that we can't even be on time. These old tortoises, well, they focus on one thing at a time, for it may be the last time they do it! As they say, "Stop and smell the roses."

We make so many stops on our journey of life, we never stop and just focus on one thing and allow that moment to be. This is why people get mad at old, slow drivers. It seems they are going slower than the posted speed limit but is that not the suggested maximum speed limit? Why is it assumed that every person on the road has to push it to the MAXIMUM limit to get somewhere?

Everything is a rush – rush – rush that it all becomes so impossible to juggle and each moment, each task becomes watered down. We lose a second here, we lose a second there, and the next thing you know, our whole life has passed us by, and we become the old person that gets passed by. And finally, when it's too late, that's when you learn to slow down – at least you've got time to pick out a sharp suit.

Ego Death & The Void

There's one day in time for me that doesn't feel like it's drifted far into the past, even though it was more than 15 years ago. A memory on repeat, unable to fade, like someone clicking "refresh" in my mind.

It all started when me and the boys had a good idea: we'd take double the recommended amount (if there is such a thing) of Magic Mushrooms.

Normally we'd eat an "eighter," which is what it sounds like: one eighth of an ounce.

But this time we decided to split an entire ounce between four people. A quarter ounce. You can know the other 'psychonauts' as Larry, Curly, and Moe.

These days, when scientists study Psilocybin, they give

their little test pigs about .3 MG. Well, I went in for 8.5G myself: two eighters, plus a gram and a half leftover from Curly's stash (he'd never done Shrooms before this night.)

Since Shrooms were hard to find, and I had a reputation for being a street shadow guide, I was always asked to join these internal voyages as a kind of 'high Sherpa' guiding my friends through the psychoactive mountain range. This was mainly because I didn't freak out and I had good walking boots.

When people did freak out, or saw spiders on the floor, I always reminded them: isn't this what you paid for? Isn't this what you wanted to see spiders all over the floor!? To melt reality. Isn't that why you paid the drug dealer, so you could have a "trip?" Well, you got it, buddy! Bon Voyage!

Shrooms ALWAYS took about 45 minutes to kick in, but on this night, we were in for a ride less than 10 minutes after taking our epic dose.

This couldn't be right, I thought to myself, Shrooms ALWAYS took 45 minutes to kick in, but I would not be driving on this trip, merely riding shotgun for 16 hours.

The effect of the extra eighter was like the difference between being tipsy with a buzz and being blackout wasted.

Shroom trips have a rainbow-like trajectory and as the mushroom poison hits your body, it takes a certain amount of time to leave. Therefore, there is always a climax, a peak. A point where you hit the highest you could be and then after that point, you start to slowly float back to reality and resume clarity.

Kind of like the effects of being sick: first, you feel it coming on, then you're at the worst point possible, then you start to feel better. Shrooms are the same way, as you are getting sick from the poison of the Shroom. (Just a side effect of the good medicine, I'd remind myself.)

As the night went on and I got higher and higher, the things that attached me to this world slowly started to drift away. The big attachment to succumb to this fading power was my ego.

The ego is that little voice you hear talking to you all the time, always 'making sense of the nonsense' going on around you. It plays an important role in your psyche: a heavy anchor keeping your sanity within the calm bay. But like any good sailor knows, sometimes you gotta ditch that anchor to find adventure.

The ego keeps track of names, ideas, rules, people's faces! The ego is not real though, not like your brain is real, at least...

If you see an unfamiliar house, you know not to go in it, because your ego has been taught the rules and knows what would happen if you did. Even though nothing is really stopping you from sneaking through a window or even trying to catch an open garage door. It is only your EGO that keeps you grounded to who, what, when, where, and why you should or shouldn't do things – it contextualizes your actions.

When they say someone has a "big ego," it means they see themselves how a drunk person sees the world! Blurred, distorted, and not true! Y'all ever see those muffin tops walkin' 'round Walmart with yoga pants on too tight? Now, that's a big ego!

Now, if something were to come between you and your ego...I don't know...say, 8.5 grams of Golden Caps...then you would start seeing through the world of rules, through the eyes of the mushroom, and not through the ego.

It's a paradigm shift, completely altering the way you view the world. Like when people realized the Earth wasn't the center of the Universe. Shrooms did the same thing to my mind!

I thought I was the center, and that everything was moving around me, but really it was I who was moving around everything!

As the night went on, Moe (whose house we were at) started to tweak a little, so he wanted to be alone and left me with Larry and Curly (the newbie) in the basement. Moe's problem was that his parents were upstairs. He began freaking out by fixating on the idea he'd let some low-lifes take this gargantuan dose of Shrooms in their home.

He decided that the best way to fix this problem was, surprisingly, to go lay down in his room for a while.

And then there were three...me, Larry and Curly, who all slowly continued our descent into 'madness' as reality and everything else we knew started to disintegrate.

Then all of a sudden, Curly's phone rang. The word "MOM" appeared on the screen. He asked me what a **"MOM"** was.

I told him I didn't know, but he best not answer it you never know who it could be!

We decided we shouldn't answer any more BEEPS because we didn't know who could be calling, and this "MOM" person, whoever it was, was just gonna have to wait till tomorrow!

I asked him in return:
"Did we take a drug earlier?"
To which he responded, "I don't remember."

As the little things that keep you attached to this reality like words start to drift away, so do other bigger things like time.

Then once time stops making sense, your ego is soon to follow. Without the ego, the mind cannot reason that time will pass. Pass into what, tomorrow? From where? How can you know of tomorrow if you have forgotten the words that hold the very ideas?

After some time of silence, Curly went to use the bathroom and before he came downstairs, he thought it would be funny to turn off the lights.

I couldn't tell you how long he had been upstairs for or how long the lights were turned off, but any fiber that grounded me to reality left with the lights. In the dark, my body disappeared. I couldn't feel it anymore.

All that I felt was my consciousness floating in...the Void.

I was in the Void.

The void is the absence of everything, like a sensory deprivation tank, and yet, paradoxically, it is everything all at once and all we can ever know. It is the true state of the Universe. This is where time, ego, and everything collapses into. The blank canvas sitting behind our realm of water colors.
I understood now that all of space is the same. The same

127

stardust space that the nuclear fusion of sun exists in, you exist in. The same space that the rings of Saturn spin in, you spin in.

All of space at its tiniest level is just one big blob and somewhere in there my body just melted into the background of this...space.

Then in that darkness, there was a blinding light, but not visual light. It was like a light inside the front of my head – almost blinding, even though we were in the dark.

It was the energy of the floating consciousness.

It felt like I was standing under blinding light and at that moment, I was at perfect peace and thankful for understanding. I understood the mushroom was something to be respected and considered, it was Good Medicine.

Therefore, I would have to stop taking the Shrooms because the life form that was the Shroom, the plant teacher, was not to be taken for granted and there was little left to show me. I had truly peered behind the curtain of reality where so few will see, and I shouldn't abuse or exploit this healing energy.

When the lights flicked back on, I was different.

I was on my knees and my hand ran along the seams of an old dusty couch that I had seen for years, but it was like I was feeling cloth for the first time. Actually, the couch wasn't that old or dusty, it was meant just how it should be.

My senses were overloaded beyond my explanation and it

was almost like they had become fried and reset. Our ego

tempers so much of our experiences that we never appreciate or take the time to experience the detail of things. We never stop to smell the roses.

So many of us forget to feel something or someone for what it actually is.

The ego is always trying to tell us what our experiences are and aren't. Before you touch or walk onto grass, you're already assuming its softness. Before you jump into a pool, you have already assumed its coldness. The old couch is assumed to be dusty. It's how some magicians can trick people into eating an onion by convincing their ego that it's actually an apple.

Sometimes you have to let go of what you think and just feel it.

Then, as I was feeling the sofa, I heard "Larry! Larry!" and I looked over to see the third man (who I had not mentioned until this point) sitting slumped in a chair, and he had puked all over his shirt.

I started to sober up and came back to reality quickly, and as the "street shaman" I indeed knew exactly what had happened... Larry had spent too much time on his own, in his own mind, with his own thoughts, without talking to us.

This whole time between the light being off and talking about taking drugs, my best friend "Curly" and I had unintentionally exiled him.

Sometimes on Shrooms, if you don't talk to anyone for long periods of time, you can drift into your own headspace so far that you can't come out of it...down the rabbit hole, as they say.

Me and some of my friends who tripped always knew this. If we were getting so high that we were in 'awe,' we would start 'shooting the shit' with each other so as not to let the other person drift away. Kinda like a "Hey, you didn't fall asleep on me, did you?"

But with time being so out the window, it was hard to tell how long we hadn't spoken to Larry for. It could have been an hour, or it could have been hours. We didn't do this on purpose, but just like normal guys do when they sit and chill, we don't always have to talk.

However, on Shrooms, you have to stay in constant communication to keep you grounded.

When that internal voice leaves you, if there is no voice at all, where does that leave you?

You know when someone's talking to you, but you didn't realize it, or were thinking about something else, and then you just kind of 'snap back to reality' and say, "Yeah, yeah" or "HUH"? Imagine that times a million...except you don't come back and it's actually times a billion.

I was in his face snapping my fingers, saying "LARRY! LARRY!" and he looked directly into my eyes and didn't even budge; he was empty as his narrow dark eyes were darting around the room.

Science calls this "Nystagmus," but I call it..."TWEAKIN' HARD."

I stood Larry up and helped him take his shirt off, so he

wasn't sitting in his vomit. And then, who should walk downstairs right at this moment...Moe.

He started crying when he saw that Larry had thrown up all over himself and the floor, because surely his parents would kill him now. Moe had just finished vomiting himself upstairs, and the only reason he came down now was because he heard us yelling (the irony being how silent we actually were.)

Larry's eyes were still darting left and right. We had all reasoned that he was wasted for the night and we should lay him down.

As we walked him over to a bed, for whatever reason, I felt like he needed a hug. I knew he had been disconnected and I figured that real human contact may bring him back to reality.

So, I gave him a big sideways hug, like an arm-around-the-neck, ole'-buddy-type hug. When I hugged him though, the space between our bodies melded away and it felt like I was one large body. I could almost feel his arm or the mass on that side, like we were some sort of conjoined twin.

The Shrooms wanted to take one more jab at me to remind me about the space between.

After that night I realized the real power of the mushrooms. The rabbit hole goes deeper than many could ever imagine.

With enough Shrooms, you'd throw up in your lap and sit in. With enough Shrooms, you'd begin to slur your words. With enough Shrooms, you wouldn't be able to talk or walk or do much of anything.

And then I got that same old thought I always got on

mushrooms: I shouldn't do drugs anymore...hadn't I learned my lesson?

The ecstasy and puking and crying and madness that came from them were all so unreal...so unnatural.

Not only would I stop taking Shrooms, but I also had to stop drinking alcohol.

When you slur your words drunk, people laugh. When you can't walk while you're drunk, people laugh.

And so, when I see these people poisoning themselves, I see a flash back in their life to a time when their parents wished for them to have these abilities. When the people who loved them the most cheered and laughed for them to walk and talk.

Now they surround themselves with people who cheer the opposite. Who laugh and cheer at our destruction.

Perfect Timing

After my trip to The Void, I wanted to share my newfound insights with some of the popular girls. Like I already told you earlier, I sat at the "popular lunch table" at school and that was probably not a good place to try and discuss the nature of reality.

The Monday after I came back from The Void, I tried telling two of the popular girls whom I ate lunch with about my revelations on time!

I slowly explained to them that life was like a clock on the wall...that even though one second clicks away at the same speed, we don't necessarily all "feel" one second pass at the same speed.

You know...time flies when you're having fun or goes really slow when you're bored!

Time is a concept. It's subjective – we all feel it differently.

Clumsy humans like to make time something we can see right in front of our eyes! We like to have evidence, we like to wear, see, and measure the time.

BUT! I won't let society 'dumb down' my life to the hands of a rigid clock, forever clicking away endlessly. Time is as alive as me and you just look at what it does.

Time flows and time stops, you can save time, lose time, have free time, and have too much time. There's Good Times & Bad Times & Best Times & Worst Times. You can be IN overtime, but not IN time, only ON time. And there is the right time and the wrong time. Time drags, time flies, and time crawls! You can be out of time, and some say we're all living on borrowed time. There IS time and THIS time and THAT time and HAVE time and ONLY time. And half time, full time, your time, our time, and every time. Many times, we say this is the time of our lives, but we do it time and time again.

And so, I told these popular girls how nothing else mattered but "time," and that the whole catch to this time thing was that you could look backwards, but not forwards for some reason.

Like someone made an imaginary block in your mind and the "forward part" was blocked from you. But the amazing thing is you could make up the "forward part" yourself, whatever you wanted - as long as you had a vision. Then, I told them the most important thing, and that was…

"The time would come."

A Beautiful Day to Die

You know in the movie *Titanic* where the band is playing music as the ship is going down?

As everyone is freaking out, kids are going left, Richies are going right, and ladies are jumping onto the rescue boats...and these guys continue to jam.

Now, I know *Titanic* was considered a "love" story, but that part was hardcore badass, *in my humble opinion*. What better way to leave this world than a gnarly jam sesh on a sinking ship? Talk about taking control of your destiny!

I say: if you've got a good, clean, noble way out – well, then let it be a beautiful day to die; what are you waiting for?

Push that little girl out of the way of the incoming car – take the bullet for the mayor - save the drowning boy! Life is worth dying for and plus, what else you got better to do?

What are you so afraid of dying for?

My uncle once told me he thought ghosts were people who held onto this world so much, their soul could never leave. The people in Limbo were just those who never got over their life here on Earth.

I hope I never leave a beautiful day in fear. My uncle told me that when my grandfather died, as he lay there, his brothers and the mariachi showed up to play him sweet Mexican music...*is that how the lowly are remembered,* I thought, *by how they die?*

Whether it be in a freak accident, disease, cancer, whatever. Most of our lives just come down to...how we die.

Bob had Cancer. Susie crashed her car. Billy OD'd.

Sure, some of us have a good little dash in between the start and end dates, but there are slim chances of a mariachi showing up for me. I heard a child talk about his death once and this little boy wanted "fireworks" at his funeral...and I can't say I disagree.

Our society can't accept death for what it is. And so, we fail to look death in the eye and see it as the only certainty we're born with: that we will all one day eventually die.

Instead, we try to fight it forever, living in fear of this eternal truth. But to live in fear of death is to never truly live. So, ironically you were dead from the start. *Nice job.*

The lowly will be lucky if the overworked and underpaid

nurse in the room turns up the tube enough for us to listen to one final fake news report before my final departure.

You really think I wanna end up drugged up and numb during "visiting hours" as my family walks in one by one on Grandpa's final thrill ride to the graveyard?

Society has taken everything else from me – I'll be dammed if I let them take my beautiful death too.

I won't let them take MY TIME to die, so I say let the sun be out, let it be raining. Whatever it is, it will surely be beautiful.

You've Got Mail

You know what I started thinking about, after all this time. This whole language is just a sham...humans should just change the way we talk.

What if we went back to Morse code and just started beeping again? Birds seem to do it just fine: chirping and communicating by sound alone. Maybe if we talked like that, we'd understand each other a lot better.

Strangely enough, I started thinking that I already spoke this Beepy language...

I first understood it when I stepped into my car and the big machine "Beeped" at me ever so nicely to put my seat belt on. It wouldn't stop "Beeping" until I did! Other times, if the machine thought it was being stolen, the alarm would sound and it would "BEEP" so loud it scared you!

Then I realized I could speak this Beepy language to other lowly drivers too. Sometimes I would give them two soft "beeps," sometimes I would blast them with a long "beep" – but both sounds meant totally different things.

Most lowly speak this Beepy language too and I've had many conversations via beep. Often when someone talks back, they may even throw up a middle finger to go with it! Some people just gotta talk with their hands, I guess...

I started to wonder...who taught me this Beepy language? My grandpa had a foghorn in his '89 Caddy and my father has been known to Beep at cars in a drive-thru, which I always thought was an English-speaking zone only. Maybe speaking Horn is something of a family tradition!

Yet I don't ever remember anybody teaching it to me, I reasoned it must have been the machines.

Because I remember a day when you got an email and the computer would say, "You've got mail!"

What happened to that?

As time went on, cars, computers, and phones all started beeping and vibrating. Even your microwave went and got itself a great "Boop."

Now the machine hivemind sends everyone one large beep known as a "STATE EMERGENCY" or "AMBER ALERT" and OHHHHH! How awful the sound when these machines make their dreadful beep all together. The Beep so awful you can't help but talk about it with everyone by asking them if they heard it too.

Then one day, I heard the most eloquent beeping I ever heard before. It was coming from the TV and was a much more complicated version of this Beepy robot language that the average lowly spoke.

It was a robot, and his name was R2D2 and the movie was Star Wars.

This little robot talked with inflections and different length beeps and boops and, by God, I could kind of understand this little robot. He was an emotional little fella too - very high anxiety!

R2D2 showed me I was much better at speaking Beep than I ever realized.

Over time, it seems as if the machines knew the best way to get our attention was to stop speaking our language and start speaking their own - the Beeps!

Now, when we die, the last thing we hear is the sound of our dying, beeping heart on the robot heartbeat machine. And as the steady beeping rhythm of our beautiful dying hearts fades away, we hear our final dead tone as the heart monitor machine chirps our most famous beep of them all...the flatline.

Zombie Nuke

Imagine walking up to a group of zombies and trying to have a conversation with them. Imagine trying to tell them they shouldn't eat brains anymore. Imagine trying to convince them they should try a vegan diet.

What do you think they would do? They'd probably give you some confused zombie look and then try to eat your brains.

Zombies automatically recognize those who are not zombies. They wboon't eat or attack other zombies – it's a zombie code.

The moral of the story is: if you act like a zombie, then you're safe. People are zombies.

Just like zombies, we feel comfortable when others around us are brainless and don't critique. Zombies don't want the truth or counter ideas; zombies just like eating brains – just like humans. Wait, no, that's not right. You get the idea though.

When the zombies find out someone is different, all the other zombies turn on them to try and devour them, then hopefully turn them into a zombie too.

Those who want to be different or to "stand out from the crowd," whether that's by wearing a pink mohawk, or reading the bible on the street, become the easiest defectors for the zombie nation to go out and feed on.

Most understand this at a basic level. When we see some guy with face tattoos complain they can't get a job...DUH!

(Everyone knows that zombies don't get face tattoos!)

Everyone also knows when you go to a party or family gathering, the zombie lowly are going to ask you a checklist of questions to see if you are acting like a good, diligent zombie.

What do you do? Are you in school? Do you have a boyfriend or girlfriend? Are you going to have kids? Have you eaten enough brains today? Wait, no, not that last one. Point is, the zombies only know how to gauge each other by lowly standards (where often the questions reveal internal expectations of the enquirer.)

Once the boxes are complete, you have become a complete zombie.

Nothing worse than telling Grandma you don't have a girlfriend for the fourth year in a row.

Zombies don't care to ask if you're happy, or if your soul is at ease, or if there is something you want to talk about. Something you need to cry about.

When I set out with the message that are these short stories, I knew I could never approach the zombie masses as the others have tried before me. If I had something meaningful I wanted to say, if I wanted to talk about Christ, I could never come out and say that because the zombies would tear me apart... I would be a fool to do what they did before me... Like True Evil, the master manipulators, I would have to blend in and act normal. Then when they let me close and thought I was a Zombie - I would tell them my ideas. When they realize I have been "playing zombie" that is when their mind is nuked. The Zombie Nuke.

I mastered my ability to blend in with the zombies, and I decided I would do all the things a zombie was expected to do, except I wanted to do it better.

So I asked myself, what if I had more friends, more money, more clothes, more cars, more girlfriends, more vacations? What if I was Super Zombie and beat every zombie checklist going?

Then could we talk about something that mattered?

Magic Mirrors

Have you ever seen someone walk by a mirror and NOT look in it?

It weirds me out to think that someone could walk by a mirror and NOT take even a little glance of themselves...what if you have a booger in your nose? What if there is food in your teeth?

Looking at mirrors has become so normal that we don't think twice about it. Do you know of any other items that can steal your attention like that, and (for some) hold them in a trancelike state? Do you find it difficult to walk past a building or car and not check your reflection? And when is the last time you saw a building or car without 'mirrors'?

Strangely enough, millions of selfies are posted across the internet showing people standing WITH their favorite mirror.

I mean, how can someone take a picture *"IN a mirror"* anyways?

We post pictures with our mirrors and inside all of us subconsciously chants that vein Disney witch: "Mirror, Mirror, on the wall, who's the fairest of them all?" I guess the internet likes shall decide.

Mirrors, no matter how normal they seem, have never been part of this natural world. All you have to do is consider what happens when almost every animal looks into one. Strangely enough, I was told my whole life IF you break one of these Magic Mirrors, then you would be doomed to eight years of bad luck. This was the highest sentencing of bad luck I ever heard of, and what a clever way to nudge behavior to preserve these mirrors and keep them infesting our world.

And so, I now ask...do you NOT know the story of Bloody Mary?

For those who know of the urban legend of Bloody Mary and not the tomato drink, you will already understand this mirror magic.

As a kid, we were taught the story of Bloody Mary: if you went into your bathroom in front of your mirror and started switching the light on and off while calling out "Bloody Mary," then you would see something in the mirror. This thrill ride taught us witchcraft at a young age..."Mirror Gazing."

Then when Harry Potter first came out, all the "religious nutjobs" cried out and tried to ban it from schools – they said it was teaching witchcraft! They said it was the workings of the occult. And you know what? Years later I saw the movies, and would you believe it, Harry is talking to his dead parents in a mirror.

In 2010 an experiment was done by the Department of Psychology at the University of Urbino in Italy. They wanted to see if the Bloody Mary phenomenon could be scientifically proven. And surprise, surprise, it was! They were able to make what they called "illusions" in the mirror in over 50 people. Lo and behold, with candlelight set up just the right way to make a shadowy, flickering dim light, they began to see faces.

Some people saw monsters, some saw random faces, and some even saw their dead family:

"All fifty participants experienced some form of this dissociative identity effect, at least for some apparition of strange faces and often reported strong emotional responses in these instances.

For example, some observers felt that the `other' watched them with an enigmatic expression a situation that they found astonishing. Some participants saw a malign expression on the `other' face and became anxious. Other participants felt that the `other' was smiling or cheerful, and experienced positive emotions in response. The apparition of deceased parents or of archetypal portraits produced feelings of silent query.

Apparition of monstrous beings produced fear or disturbance. Dynamic deformations of new faces (like pulsations or shrinking, smiling or grinding) produced an overall sense of inquietude for things out of control.

At the end of a 10-minute session of mirror gazing, the participant was asked to write what he or she saw in the mirror.

The descriptions differed greatly across individuals and

included: (a) huge deformations of one's own face (reported by 66% of the fifty participants); (b) a parent's face with traits changed (18%), of whom 8% were still alive and 10% were deceased; (c) an unknown person (28%); (d) an archetypal face, such as that of an old woman, a child, or a portrait of an ancestor (28%); (e) an animal face such as that of a cat, pig, or lion (18%); (f) fantastical and monstrous beings (48%)."

Black Mirrors

I like to ask people if they know what a black mirror is.

A lot of them know it is a popular show on Netflix, but they had never really considered what an actual "black mirror" was.

So, I tell them that a black mirror is something used in witchcraft, sometimes used to see faraway places or people. The old wizards and witches called them "Scrying" mirrors.

Frighteningly, black mirrors are what all screens become when you turn them off! Whether it be a computer monitor, cell phone, iPad, calculator, or TV. When the power goes off, you quickly see the black mirror for what it is. If you look close enough, you may even be able to see your own dark reflection faintly staring back at you.

Imagine if we thought of "TV SCREENS" more like "DOOR

SCREENS" whether the screen is on or open will determine what can come through.

No different than a witch looking into a crystal ball when you look into a black mirror, you too can now see things through the open screen and can have sight into faraway places and people that are not within your sight, your vision, or your reality.

We use the remote control to change the channel on the medium of television.

Witches are mediums that can control black mirrors to channel visions remotely.

Such a powerful magical item in our homes, without any thought or judgment, or anyone thinking twice!

And like the magic mirror, there is no item more hypnotizing.

The black mirrors are so powerful that laws have been made to restrict what kinds of images and visions you can channel through these mirrors.

Images of murder and child and animal abuse are legally too lewd and disgusting to be shown on these mirrors. Yet True Evil uses these very black mirrors to record their dark ways.

Ohhhh! How have we ended up in a world full of mirrors!?

Sadly, there is a scary idea in this world: that you could brainwash entire generations of low-lows and, not only could you brainwash them, but you could also make them love the very thing responsible. A real Stockholm Syndrome.

Just look and see for yourself on Black Friday how the lowly fight tooth and nail for more black mirrors. They fight over the TVs and computers, cell phones and laptops. The very black mirrors that told them they needed more! The lowly now love the very things that have brainwashed them, the very things that have us under their spell: The Black Mirrors.

Toilet Martyr

I like to ask people if, when they go into a public bathroom...do they make a "nest?"

What's a nest, they ask?

A nest is when you lay toilet paper down around the toilet seat before you promptly sit on it like a bird in its nest. Sometimes at airports or other government buildings, they will have a premade nest ready for you.

And for the most part, most people are nesters. Even for me, it is kind of tacky not to make a nest!

But what strikes me as funny is that...a little bit of toilet paper is all it takes for people to feel safe. That's it! A quarter inch of ass wipe and that's what helps them sleep at night.

Now don't get me wrong, I am not unreasonable. I am not going to walk into a blown out porta-potty and raw dog it. I have reason, BUT please don't call me crazy for putting my faith in God, when you'd rather put yours in some toilet paper!

Don't call me crazy when I say God comes with me everywhere I go – even into the shitter!

Now I go to the gym and they have a paper towel to wipe down the seats. Locks to protect your clothes. Safety shutoffs in case you fall off the machine and security cameras to watch it all!

We don't even know what we fear anymore!

Is it germs? Is it ourselves? Is it a thief? Who knows!
There's never any end to man's attempt to protect himself from his own fears.

Then, in 2020, when the Coronavirus hit, everyone began to buy out toilet paper and no one could explain why people were doing it - rather than storing other more obvious necessities like food and bad medicine.

It was because they turned to the only thing they have ever had faith in, the only thing that's ever made them feel safe: Toilet Paper.

Somewhere deep in people's hearts, they had more faith in toilet paper than they did God, and when shit hit the fan, in a godless society where Big Brother couldn't give them an answer, they turned to the only thing they had faith in: Toilet Paper.

So, let it be said; if I die on the toilet from NOT making a nest, then so be it.

If God wishes to make an example of me that I die such a miserable death by evil, wretched germs, then so be it.

I will be the Toilet Martyr.

The Age of Magic & Science

If Harry Potter makes a potion that can change what he looks like, we call it magic, but if the Hulk makes a serum that changes who he is, well, then we call it science! Really, they are one and the same - only the word has changed. Or as others have put it: magic is just science that we don't understand yet.

For me to explain this idea, I should tell you of the first time I went to Universal Studios.

I was shocked at all the incredible technology they had...I mean, they really pulled out all the stops: I'd never seen anything like it. Everything was so convincing and realistic, if I were a kid, I would surely think it's all real.

But the funny thing I noticed was that this park (which we paid an arm and a leg to enter) was no different to the world we already lived in. Sure, sure, Universal Studios was a lot flashier, with a lot of 'movie magic' tech lying around. The ideas supposedly were out of this world, but the explanation of everything was subtly right before my eyes!

From "Jurassic Park" to "Men in Black" dinosaurs to aliens. Films answered all the questions we could have about what was before and what will come after. Then when they introduced Harry Potter's world and MARVEL's universe, I knew we were in the age of magic and science!

Just look at Star Wars! Wow! Now that place really had magic and science figured out.

Ask yourself why Star Wars is so different than all the other scifi material out there. How has Star Wars become "cultural" and everything else fodder for Trekkies and nerd fan boys?

Well, because Star Wars understands magic and science! Both the physical and spiritual, this truth we live in. It doesn't matter how far you go into the future or into space, there will always be Good vs. Bad. Star Wars successfully taps into this timeless truth of these irreducible concepts.

It doesn't matter how much science there is. This is the fundamental truth that we never escape, that underneath it all is a force we cannot see, Good vs. Bad. Dark Side vs. Light Side.

The Jedi are what separate the Star Wars universe from everyone else. These characters can use "the force," an invisible energy that they can control to manipulate reality outside the realm of scientific understanding. The Magi, I mean Jedi, do magic in a universe based on science.

Star Wars isn't a story about science in the future; it is a story about magicians in the future - sorcerers in space. Space Wizards, if you will. You're a Wizard, Harry Wan Kenobi!

Of course, it makes sense, that MARVEL and Star Wars, the imagineers of our science futures, would be bought and directed by Disney, the Magic Kingdom itself.

I was raised on the Magic School Bus, and a MARVEL universe, which started with science like IRONMAN. The modern Prometheus, the final work of a scientific mad man. Yet even MARVEL has turned into a universe that has seen the likes of THOR and Dr. Strange. Characters and gods who exist on pure magic with no attempts of explanation within the boundaries of a scientific universe.

The MARVEL universe isn't a story about billionaire scientists saving our planet with science. It is a revelation of the magical universe we already live in and the limitations science faces against these greater spiritual forces.

If Dr. Strange makes a portal, we call it magic. If Luke Skywalker does it, we call it science. There is no difference; magic is just science unknown.

A few months later, I went to the great capital of Washington, DC and found that all the museums there were free...and they were spinning the same stories of where we came from, and where we will go. I guess indoctrination is priceless!

Propaganda, if you will. *Just another DC Universe.*

In the Capital's museums, the Smithsonian showed prehistoric dinosaurs, monkey men, and advanced "alien

-looking" technology – telling us that this is what life used to look like and this is what life will look like. It was the same story they were spinning at the "fictional" Universal Studios, except the Capital didn't show the part where the monkey men turn into highly evolved mutant X-Men.

They showed their advanced telescopes and microscopes that used magic mirrors to see beyond the veil, beyond what the eye could see, and still they called it science.

Strange that the magical goblins in the Harry Potter world used scientific telescopes like they showed in the Aerospace Museum...I thought humans had invented this technology.

Even stranger then that inside this place of good we call Universal Studios, they had a place called "Voodoo Doughnuts," where they sold donuts with a pentagram and other devil-worshipping symbols. I think True Evil has set up shop there, and it's doing a roaring trade like its buddies in the Capital.

The Cost of Friendship

Most people from Southeast Michigan, by Detroit, have a similar understanding that some, if not most, parts of the city are not safe at night and the general rule of thumb is you don't idle there for long. Even if, for a moment, you find yourself stopped at a red light...you should GO.

I would also go as far to say that people actually from Detroit are not like people from the suburbs surrounding Detroit. As Eminem so eloquently said, "Now everybody...claimin' Detroit, when y'all live 20 miles away." Well, that was true. The people who were really from Detroit were a lot more violent and had a lot less to lose than the suburban kids who acted like they were from the city.

One night me and Curly, decided that we would go and do some 'bar hopping' and see what was going on. I myself had purposely not drank that night, as I was aware of the dangers of being drunk or out of control in the hostile environment that *is* Detroit. As we walked along the sidewalk, we saw a party bus pulled over in the street, in front of a few bars. From and around the bus, there was a group of about 20 people openly fighting in the street. It was a lowly royal rumble of sorts and, in typical Detroit fashion, it was assumed that the police would not be coming to bring order any time soon. Quickly I realized there was a gang of hooligans beating up whatever individuals their hivemind locked in on. There was a collective group of about 15 that were teamed up. The gang was all colors and sizes, only bound by its desire for destruction.

The beatings went on for so long that a circle of spectators had formed around the kids that were fighting. And like most spectators, my buddy Curly had pulled out his phone to record videos of the battle. The outer circle all laughed and recorded until one of the gang members quickly turned on the crowd and said:

"What the fuck are you recording?"

The people to the left of Curly turned quickly to look in at him, and the people to the right of Curly turned left to look in at him. I thought the guy was speaking to everyone in the crowd, but somehow the crowd had unanimously decided that Curly was indeed the one he was talking to.

Curly was put into the spotlight of the crowd and in a split second and with some liquid courage, he had decided he would not be made a fool in the small public eye that watched.

Quickly, Curly responded, "None of your fucking business!" And that's all it took. Like magic words. Fighting words in Detroit.

You could say something like that in the Suburbs and get away with it, but in the D, that was an open invitation for fisticuffs.

I also learned the power of pulling a Black Mirror on someone that night. *Today, shooting someone with your camera is worse than shooting them with a gun.*

Before Curly could finish his sentence, the guy had both hands on his shoulder like a bouncer ready to bounce, and now Curly and this random hooligan were pushing and shoving.

In my sobriety, I didn't jump in at first. It was a 1 v 1 and Curly wanted to act tough – he got it. Now, he had to deal with the repercussions of his big mouth. Maybe this guy would teach him a useful lesson, I thought.

After about 45 seconds of tussling, Curly began to lose the fight. He was pushed into the wall and then Curly pushed back in a fit of rage, only to find himself pulled across the sidewalk and slammed into a parked car. There he was pinned for a while, then the shoving and pushing turned into punching. Now, Curly began to lose the fight very badly. The hooligan's punches bounced his head off the corner of the car while me and the rest of the crowd watched on. Everyone still recording as Curly now became the star of the newest Black Mirrors episode.

When the first thug came over to confront the crowd, it seemed as if he walked so far away from his friends that he was almost like an ember drifting away from a campfire. I never thought this little spark was a threat or would set about the blaze that followed.

As more punches dribbled his head off the aluminum, the sharks nearby must have sniffed blood in the water, and I watched as the 1 v 1 was about to turn into a gang bang. Now, someone had come behind Curly and put their arm around his neck and any sort of defense he was making with his wildly flailing arms was nullified. I could see two more guys walking over to join in the traditional Detroit-style jumping.

In an instant, my world was turned upside down. Like Spiderman who lets the criminal go because it's not his problem - only to find out moments later that the criminal would kill his uncle. The situation had escalated out of control, and now Curly was in serious danger.

In my sobriety I had a million thoughts flash through my head and time slowed down for only the second time in my life. My sixth sense kicked in and I knew now I was in a fight-or-flight situation.

Me and Curly had no business being in Detroit and the bars had now slammed their black security fences up that they use at night, locking all the people in the bar. Everyone outside was left to fend for themselves and to scrap against the bus of thugs. We were locked out so fast, it was clear that this was standard operating procedure for the bars in this area, and now it was us two vs Detroit.

With no one to help Curly and nowhere to hide, I consciously asked myself if I should just let the wolves tear him apart. No one knew I was with him; the gang thought he was alone, which made him easy prey. As much as anyone else could tell, I was just someone on the outside watching and recording. Curly would never know if I just acted like a coward and let him take his beating. He earned it - he shouldn't have said shit, and he was so drunk. I could have said, "I tried."

161

But I always walk away from a good flight.

I knew that to leave Curly alone in the hands of those guys would mean serious injury, and honestly, maybe even death. These guys were not looking to simply rough someone up, they were looking to maim someone. I knew to leave Curly alone would mean to be a coward and go against everything I stood for. Good has to stand up in the face of Bad, or else it cannot be called Good.

I decided fight.

and I hope someone would do the same for me one day.

That is, risk their life and health to go against the odds to try and save a friend. This was the cost of friendship.

Even against overwhelming numbers, if I couldn't pay the cost when I was due, then how could I ever expect someone to pay it forward for me when I needed it? To save Curly's life – this was the cost of friendship.

With no time to spare as two more guys walked around the car to make it a 4 v 1 against Curly, it was decided.

All in all, it probably took me two seconds to make the fight-or-flight decision, but when your sixth sense kicks in and time slows down, you are able to make critical decisions much quicker - like Spidey sense.

And if I were to enter this war, it had to be on the same terms as them and that I had to come with cruel intentions.

They were committed to hurting my friend, so I had to commit myself to hurting them. I had to tip the scales and go all in. Everything I had ever learned from hurting Goofball and trying to make reasonable decisions that safeguarded my life was now about to go out the window. Fighting meant to embrace the chaos. I often hear MMA fighters say they feel free in the cage, and when you decide to drop to that animalistic level and think with that primitive mind, in many ways you do become free.

I knew that if I was going to die, I would at least take one of them to hell with me and it was easily decided: it would be the one that put his hands on my friend in the first place.

He was still taking shots at Curly's face as the guy from behind him held him. I reared back like a wild stallion, like someone would crow hop a baseball. Taking two steps forward and with all my momentum from the shadows of the spectators, I "sucker punched" him. *He never saw it coming.*

From behind his right shoulder, I hit him perfectly in his bald head, square on the temple. It was a perfect homerun shot, and today I still reminisce about that perfect bullseye I hit him with. Instantly he dropped like a sack of potatoes and now, one was down.

Instantly I heard "Get that motherfucker" and they dropped Curly to the ground and started coming at me. *I took aggro.*

It seemed like before I could even take a step, the guys from around the car were now on me. I didn't think twice, and I grabbed one by the hips. Still to this day, I don't know why I grabbed him by the hips, or how it worked, but I bent him backwards at the waist with sheer adrenaline alone. I bent him backwards and he fell back, hitting his head on the curb. I had now taken out two. That's when I felt someone kick me in my back. Then I got punched in the back of the head and kicked in the rib. I was now on my knees and, like a gladiator refusing to die, I was kicked again in the back, the second kick forcing me over into a turtle position on the ground. There I lay hunched over - and I felt the barrage of kicks landing on my side and the back and top of my head. I just kept telling myself, *don't get knocked out.* I knew from previous fights, generating enough energy and leverage to knock somebody out in the turtle position is tough when their head is tucked between their legs. I held my hands over the back of my head and tried to prevent myself from getting knocked out. I kept telling myself, just make sure you don't get knocked out, because then you will really have no way to protect your head. And if I couldn't protect my head, well, then I could expect brain damage.

I'm not sure how long I got jumped for, but I had survived. I pushed back to my feet with renewed vigor and a sense that I could not be taken out so easily, I looked around only to see no one around me. *Was I concussed?* The bus was gone and two guys on the street watching said:

"Damn, homie, you held it down." Their validation at my inclination for violence made me feel "cool." I was excited - frenzied even.

My shine was quickly sobered up, when I saw that Curly was concussed bad and was not as excited as me. There was one other kid who lay face down unconscious in front of one of the other bars. The patrons in the bar still locked inside watched and screamed behind a fence looking out on the city streets at the Mad Max Dystopia, as a few stragglers outside called for 911.

The gang had truly left damage in its wake, and in this case a victim, a casualty. I said a prayer for that kid because I knew no one else would and I prayed he would wake and be okay. I had seen this too many times before and I felt vindicated, believing I saved Curly from that same fate. *If only this other kid had a friend, I thought, maybe he wouldn't be there face down in the street.*

Curly also looked as if he was in the wake of this tornado that ripped through the people. His face was covered in blood, and his shirt was ripped and torn. He was concussed and in his drunken state, he could not make sense of anything. I put his arm around my shoulder, and we walked him out of the warzone that was Detroit. We had a friend, who lived in Detroit and this could be a safe house for the night - if we could make it there. *Out of the oven and into the frying pan, as they say.*

As we walked by the hardened characters of Detroit they were gleeful to see this "pretty little white boy" beaten up and blood ridden. They all said, "Damn, homie, you got fucked up," and they laughed in his face at the drunken bloody mess he was. *Classic Schadenfreude.*

I was mad at Curly for some time after that. For him, it was a memory that he didn't remember. Just a crazy drunken night. He said, "You'll never let me forget that," but I think it's because I'll never forget that.

See, what Curly didn't know is I had a knife in my pocket the whole time. I was so prepared to handle any situation I got myself into that night, I would have never guessed that it would be someone else who dragged me into it. When I was on the ground taking that beating for the both of us, I thought about going for that knife. I guess you can say me and those other kids are lucky I didn't do that. You know how easy it would have been for me to pull that knife out and start swinging? No, instead, I took my ass whoopin' straight that night because I guess I lied; I really wasn't ready to kill.

The next morning, even though my back and head were sore from the beating, I just hoped I didn't give that lowly man I sucker punched brain damage...

The End

Appendix

Bed Crumbs - A small amount or quantity given.
"My paycheck was bed crumbs."

Big Ears - A name for a person eavesdropping or listening far away.
"Be quiet, Big Ears is listening."

Big Man - A name for a person in charge, boss or manager.
"You better go tell the Big Man, you fucked up."

Bubbleguts - When you're constantly farting and pooing.
"I got the Bubbleguts...bad!"

Buddy Hungee - A wedgie noticeable in a public place. Reference alluding to a pair of buttocks hungrily eating its own pants.
"That Buddy Hungee."

Buggers - A group of people who are constantly annoying you.
"Leave me alone, Buggers!"

Crop Dusting - The act of farting on someone secretly. Usually happens after a bad case of the Bubbleguts.
"I think he's gonna Crop Dust those lowlows..."

Crotch Rot - The funk accumulated around a person's genitalia after a long sweaty day.
"I got Crotch Rot."

Deadbeat & Deady - A name for a person with no life or soul. Someone who gives 5% effort.
"What a Deadbeat, I can't believe this Deady!"

Dippy Doo - Can also be used as Dip and Dippy. A person of low intelligence.
"Watch out for the Dip crossing the street!"

Dirty Bird - A person who is nasty or does disgusting things.
"Did that Dirty Bird just Cropdust those Dippys"

Dragon Breath - A person with persistent, unpleasant odor breath. Can also be pronounced DRAGOONE Breath.
"Go get a whiff of that Dirty Birds, Dragon Breath..."

Dumbo - Another name for Eavesdropping." A person who hears everything.

"Dumbo heard you."

Flunkee - A Deady who does low-level Dippy work.

"Stop being a Flunkee."

Fuschi Face - More modernly known as "Resting Bitch Face"

"She has her Fuschi Face on. "

Goof Ball - A person who does unthought of things.

"He was acting like a Goofball."

Horse Face - A person who is unpleasant to look at, possibly due to an uncanny resemblance to a horse.

"Who, Horse Face?"

Low-Low - Usually a Dirty Bird who is lower than low.

"Look at that Low-Low!"

Mimi Dare - A term for going to sleep. In reference to the sound cartoon characters make when they sleep...(Meemee-meemeemee)

"Mimi Dare for me."

Not All There - A passive term for Lowlows who are acting like Goofballs indicating that their mental faculties are not all at once 'present and correct.'

"Not all there."

Numbnuts - A derogatory term for a Lol-low

"Stop being such a Flunkee, Numbnuts!"

Scag - An older lady who often wears her Fuschi Face.

"The Scags back."

Split Buzz - A term for when you want someone to leave you alone.

"Split Buzz, Buggers."

Starey - A person who constantly looks at you without care.

"What are you looking at, Starey!"

Stick Bones - A person of long and skinny stature.

"Where's Stick Bones?"

Stoneface - Another variation of Fuschi Face, with less beauty.

"Oh my, that Scag has got her Stoneface"

Strange Brew - When a Dippy or Goofball acts oddly.
"What are you doing, Strange Brew?"

Thinkies - A term for over analyzing and being critical of every situation.
"I got the Thinkies"

Throwing - A discreet term for having to use the bathroom in public, specifically a number 2. Can also be said that one is going to Play Ball.
"I gotta Throw"

Twistoid - A name for a Low-low who has oddball tendencies. Can also be used in the present form of TWISTER to accuse someone of masturbation.

"What were you doing in the shower so long, Twisting?"

Yuck Mouth - A person who has had Dragon Breath for a long period of time and has developed more than bad breath but also a thin film of residue around their lips.

"He's got Yuck Mouth."

About the Author

Daniel was born In San Diego, California & Raised in Detroit, Michigan. He has 1 girlriend, 1 brother, 2 parents, 2 cats and 5 fish.

Connect with me online:

www.thedaysofdaniel.com
Instagram: @The.Days.of.Daniel
DaysofDanielBook@gmail.com